bunny and shark

FIRST EDITION

The production of this book was made possible through the generous
assistance of the Canada Council for the Arts and the Ontario Arts Council.

 Canada Council Conseil des Arts
for the Arts du Canada

Library and Archives Canada Cataloguing in Publication

Piercy, Alisha, 1972-, author
    Bunny and shark / Alisha Piercy. -- First edition.

(Department of narrative studies)
Issued in print and electronic formats.
ISBN 978-1-77166-051-8 (pbk.).--ISBN 978-1-77166-062-4 (html)

    I. Title. II. Series: Department of narrative studies

PS8631.I4728B86 2014   C813'.6   C2014-904782-7
                                          C2014-904783-5

PRINTED IN CANADA

This is weird!
(For Jess!)

bunny
and
shark

ALISHA PIERCY

BOOKTHUG
DEPARTMENT OF NARRATIVE STUDIES
TORONTO, MMXIV

Prelude

SHE LISTENS TO THE SOUND of another mouth breathing fast. As if running. "Who is this? How did you get my number?" She butts out her cigarette so she can hold the phone with both hands.

"Hello?" And pulls the receiver away from her ear because on the other end, somewhere out there in the lowlands, where the wind has that particular note of heave, the other phone hits the ground with a crash.

She puts the receiver down on the table and stares at the mouthpiece leading to the dull, beige cord as it dangles and bobs out from the wall. She is transfixed by the disappearance of the caller's voice: a woman whose words slur together into a whisper for help. The tiny black holes spit distant sounds of rocks cracking and then a yell. Now a man's voice. Jablonsky wonders if she should hang up and press *69. Or call the police. But to say what? Her eyes flit from the silent, resting phone to her impotent reflection on the black patio window. She is waiting for the woman to come back to the phone to tell her what to do. But no one speaks.

She picks it up again and winds the curling cord around her fingers. Where, exactly, is this happening? She stops everything, every move, and lets the house settle around her. She tunes in and hears waves crashing. But that sound could be coming from her own balcony, the sea is everywhere when you're on an island. Jablonsky circles her kitchen twice, aware of herself, safe and sound in her mountainside villa, far from the panic of feet skidding down rocks and into the sands of the difficult lowland terrain.

From across the room she yells: "Hello? Are you there?" On the other end, and what she doesn't perceive: an intake of breath, as if in surprise. Not the woman. The phone goes dead.

///

You fall. Clumsy-bodied, running through the air, as if there might actually be some place to go other than over the cliff and into the sea.

Your clothes puff out, a sandal falls, and you enter the sea. You kick off the other shoe underwater and grasp at the surface. At whatever end is up in all that deep, green blackness. The night is dark but there is a sliver of moon.

"You bastard!" you scream, but it's smothered by water. Your face pushes to the surface, ragged and salted. And it occurs to you where you are, and what you've been thrown to.

You scream unstifled this time. Through the black eye he dealt you, you see him in double and fuzzy. Above, unsteady on the rocks, his white shirt blowing and his knife hung low at his side, slicing its way towards you as if you are still in front of him. Falling to his knees, terrified, he is making his way to the edge. He looks over it, afraid. That now you might not die.

Swim out of this, swim away. Or go deeply underwater. You aren't sure because no matter what you do, he's up so high, he'll see you doing it.

The horror dawns on you of having been dropped into the sea where it pushes at a right angle to the wall of cliff. Striations of brown-black rock run in endless lines all leading upwards to the bastard who won't help you. The stern sweep back down to the dark surface of sea conceals so many ways you could now die. You cry out in one final burst: "Help me!" Then you thrash for murder, carving the sea with all your limbs. Your clothes claw at you. Your face bleeds in aimless strings. You scream and whine and choke, then beg softly, your mouth going underwater, speaking halfway into the sea. You give the bastard your swan song.

Then you rest, blowing bubbles.

Don't breathe so hard, you tell yourself. No more bubbles. Go softer. Go still. Count to ten. And sink slowly under.

For some reason, being underwater makes everything stop. You feel the quiet of airless entombment. Like you are caked in warm wax.

You pray he believes it.

Swim as hard as you can in any direction deep underwater. Hold your breath. Longer, if possible, then crouch. Your arms paddle at your sides to stop you from floating up through the surface. You come up anyhow, fighting primal urges: don't choke or gasp for air. Don't see me, please don't see me. Just barely holding. Above: the see-through wall of water. Your mouth: punched and swollen but somehow controllable, shapes itself to the surface to breathe through a straw-sized O. Salt-stings as you stare through the two-inch film of green ocean glaze to see if he still sees you. You hope you seem dead. Your breath shallows to nothing as the bastard turns into a ripple of white on the cliff, looking, squinting to see, the rocks skidding under him and spilling over the edge. Play dead. Don't corpses go dead-man's-float? he'll be thinking. He won't be sure.

So you play dead for him, one last performance, lolling up and over like a seal to give him his final picture. You wait for the sound of his car. You wait for it to rear up and burn away over the lowlands.

God love him at least for believing in the myth and efficacy of the island's shark pit.

///

Their noses butt upward under the bright night waves. They make splashy peaks. Fierce, almost glittery: we've arrived! Startled, you hack and swallow water. You look from side to side. Flashes of shiny grey in every direction. They slow down to a thudding, a dissonant shark-timing of drive-bys, seemingly not yet ready to kill. Yes: to kill you! Torpedo lurches. A thunderbolt lunge that bumps you, hurts you. Then below, in dull ominous skin, tunnelling one by one.

Cold now. Getting tired already. The sharks' fins and

tails lash about in a front line that arcs wide to encircle you. Their loud slap on the water. You raise your head. I hear you, I hear you, you say to the bottom of the ocean. Their position shifts, they get closer. Just how many are there? What's needed to kill one woman? Reconfiguring, looting without actually touching. Maybe it's not you they prey on. Or they're teasing their way towards a gradual kill. You count to five, shut your eyes. Open them. See hundreds. Or so it seems. Whitecaps and moonlight mix up light with action. Was that slap the signal to attack?

Tearing your good eye away from them is next to impossible. They require that you observe every painstaking move they make. But for a second you turn to see the edge of the cliff. Could the bastard have had a heart, and turned back to hoist you out of all this?

The whole mass of ocean rising and falling, shifting you and the circle from one full sea depth high, to low, then to high again.

Something in the tone shifts from menace to release. Heavy eyelids, you let your lashes fall into your cheeks where they congeal with the blood.

Salt-choked whisper: a way out? Give into it? Give in to death and maybe it'll hurt less?

Moments before you knew he would push you over the edge, the same silent plea was cast out of your mouth like a shot. You would have been a silhouette standing there, shivering against the sea, as he backed away holding his knife. He wouldn't have seen the violence of the question. Or that you were already resigned to knowing there wasn't a way out. Not with him.

Shining, misshapen face turning from fin to fin. Waves follow waves, you watch them as you start to sink, and it occurs to you that this is about making your entire body disappear. To be made dead but also to be eaten. Will you die before being swallowed?

You put your head down on the sea, willing it, wishing it, to be a pillow.

To stand still in the sea is a marathon.

With each swell you're brought closer to the dark craggy rocks. They become an attitude, a rejection of you. They continue to put you in your place by luring you towards them. You don't dare touch them, and yet, the slower you move, the more you want to reach out your hand.

The circle gathers tightly, waxen bodies sloughing the waters. There is something playful or indignant in them, like children made to wait too long. Let's get on with it! They are clear of purpose but somehow delayed in carrying it out. No need now to catch your attention, they're plotting their angle on you. Discussing who gets what.

Your mouth pours out the last of its strangulated anxiety, somehow bringing you breath. You debate one death over the other: to be smashed against the rocks or to be eaten alive? Smashed against the rocks or eaten alive. Smashed. Eaten.

Your legs gallop in slow-motion, your arms following off-sync.

They are trying to exhaust you. To tire you out like those dogs that lope gently through the desert for days until their prey turns into a rag, and practically begs to be taken.

Keep treading. The ridiculousness of your legs doing the egg-beater in time with your chattering teeth.

Blood-mouthed, a slurry sent in the direction of the cliff: "How much longer?" You inhale saltwater. Cough. Gag. You feel the sweat of the sea beading up inside you. A ripple of shiny eyes waves through the blackness, a message from one to another, and, as if in answer, a head rears back and a black eye, round like a dove's, comes so close it fills your field of vision. You smell the reek. Its pure, invested violence. Bud rot in its teeth, a dull slab of flesh coming towards you but then falling away. Being pushed out by others.

And you realize that the circle, the steady, floating, waiting ring you've been part of for all these many minutes, is not made up of sharks, but of dolphins.

///

Dolphin-saved.

In that mysterious way dolphins do: by surrounding a human to protect it against a lone shark. As simple as that, they slap at the water in grand unison with their tails and whisk you away.

From head to toe, buzzing, you are a hum, a human with the sea, not against it.

You groan at the impossibility of it. You cry out through your salt-racked throat. Your heart wells with love for daylight. You'll see it again! Your body and the sea are a combined freedom, swimming harmoniously, as you always have, as, dolphin after dolphin, you are nudged forward, out of the trap of the cove and into open water.

In a haze of time you will never be able to pin down, you reach the shore without ever having taken a good hard look at your saviours.

///

When you open your good eye again it's to meet a blazing, round sun. You're lying in the ditch of a muddy road. Somehow, in your stupor, you made your way to the gate of one of the white mansions and buried yourself in the low-lying foliage that spreads over its tough, sandy lawn.

Without thinking, you get up and start to jog away. In which direction? Not to the roads, no, the bastard would have driven night and day to cool his rage and to banish you or your ghost. You know few people in this neighbourhood. The gates are high and barbed. It's not safe to knock on any doors. And what would you say? The bastard is king in these lands.

Anyhow, there is your body to attend to. Your crippling desire for water. It makes your movements erratic. So you limp and zigzag, careful to stay to the verge of the road.

Day one dead

*(In which Bunny curls up to the sea
and the bastard's sailboat.)*

NIGHT BRINGS DARKNESS all of a sudden on the islands.
The boaters are watching the giant cruisers make grand
parades of themselves as they cross under the bridge. Everyone throws water balloons back and forth, from boat
to bar, bar to boat, as the bridge rises and falls. It happens
every day at five. Barefoot and with a black eye, among the
happy-hour crowd, you're daring to stand out too much.
You duck in and out from behind parked cars, not seeing

anyone you recognize. You run down the narrow road that leads to the house of the Authorities where Coke-Bottle works.

Directly opposite the Authorities, the lobster-seller in the shade of a palm. The man you've known for years sits in the damp garden sheltered by an overhang of tangled trees. You've stood at the periphery of this garden many times before, peering into what is often mistaken for a doghouse. A lobster pool, in fact. The bastard always waited in the car with his sunglasses on, even at night, while you made the transaction with the lobster-seller, a preparation for dinner for the group at your house, your pretty pink villa set deep in the mountainside. Always lavish fair.

You picture the bastard as he must be now: in a clean outfit, pacing along the vast balcony, staring out to the point where he pushed you over.

What will the group say to the bastard tonight after he's expertly shucked all the oysters, after he's readied each course purely for the love of showing off? What will they say when, after all, you aren't there to serve them? "Where is Bunny?" they will ask, confused.

You, smiling enormously as you always did, your tanned hands covered in rings, doling out champagne. "Hey there Bunny-honey," they'd say. And swat you on your ass, too big to be a Playboy ass anymore, your fat ass. Your fingers, long and lacquered, dealing cash and cards faster than lightning, would run slow trails over their suit-ed shoulders as you leaned into them at the table, wafting each one with perfumed cleavage, entrancing them with your passing constellation of diamonds.

While you mesmerized them, those eager ass-swatters sunk everything, all their millions, into staying on the is-land, and inch by inch, devoured its lands. They paid the big-boss, the bastard, and you, Bunny, for a life's worth of protection. All of you drunk with collusion and the promise of isolation and everlasting wealth.

Which way out of this?

Chief Authority Coke-Bottle: the bastard's friend and a regular at the house. You are counting on it, that he is at your villa this very second, brandy snifter in hairy hand, oversized oculars half-closed and tipped up to your faux-finish ceiling. The golden liquid sliding, again and again, down his throat. The shell-sculpted mirrors reflect-ing him everywhere.

You stand outside the Precinct, not sure what to do. Dwarf palms blow around your legs. The lobster-seller doesn't even see you, you are crouching now, seeing Coke-Bottle's face multiply itself endlessly, you can't shake it. Taking your chances, you run to the Precinct door, catch a whiff of the dogs loose on the road, and pull the door open. Feel the air conditioning.

The room is informal and overly bright. Even if Coke-

Bottle isn't here, the other officers will report that some white woman was claiming her husband tried to kill her. Coke-Bottle will know.

Your bad eye pulses harder than the fluorescents, but the black men who wait know how to ignore you and yet see everything. Still, you find yourself standing there trying to hide.

An old man waves pensioner's papers to no one, to his god likely. Beside him another of the bastard's cohorts: the Italian's live-in maid, glancing your way. Impossible. She looks away like a puppet string yanked her head. You turn heel at the magazine stand, change your mind and sit down with your back to the room. The attendant glances up from his desk, says nothing, and you hear sounds of people behind him, in the offices far off, putting on jackets, changing shoes, rustling car keys. Getting ready to go home. You think: just stand up and walk back out into the balmy air.

Rushing outside, you plant yourself behind a nearby parked car. Coke-Bottle's voice growls something as the Precinct door swings open. He pulls a stream of laughter, his and others', out into the hot night. His presence is so enormous you have time to hide within the echo of his scattering reverberations. Then hear plain as day his voice again, this time speaking quietly into his cellphone: "No, no signs. Seems everything is going to be alright for you, but yeah, yeah, I'll keep an eye out. Yeah, yeah, cool it, they've been notified. Bunny's good as dead, pal."

Coke-Bottle's car drives away as you make your way down the beach road. The lobster-seller doesn't miss a beat of his hum-song, but raises an eyebrow. The hot skin of your feet on asphalt is electric, transporting you, inch by inch, back towards the water, where you were delivered. A miracle, the dolphins, no question. Sustain this, please. You can't handle the real of this yet. The let-down of walking on the ground, the dead-heavy slowness of it. The dolphins made a cradle for you, just go back there to them, to where you're protected. You deserve to be protected, you were born to that.

The smell of takeout goes by, something fried, devoured, discarded, a crumple in your ear. Girls in gold earrings as large as baskets hang around, their laughter mixing with the smell of the food you couldn't buy if you wanted to. Reaching the end of the road, you glance towards a garbage bag that looks just put out. Beside it, a pair of shoes. They are the hearty, lace-up leather kind worn by older live-in maids. The shoes fit you perfectly.

Light-headed when you lift yourself up from the street after putting them on, you think: now I can at least walk somewhere. But you're not sure where to go without any money. You don't even have a purse to carry so that it looks like you have money.

You reach the end of another small road, one leading to the beach by the bay. All locals here. You'll only be able to stay by night in these parts. Tonight you'll sleep tucked up next to the abandoned house. First you walk your new shoes right over the steep ledge of sand and sit down there to listen. Not so far out from the shore you see a number of anchored sailboats: Coke-Bottle's sleek black vessel, the Italian's blue, the bastard's newly painted red and white. Your eye is now all closed up and quiet and you stare for a long time at those haunted emblems of the men who will continue to sit at your dinner table. Until your one good eye becomes exhausted, loses focus, and with it the facts of the boats and the reality of the distances that surround you. You see your own boat shape-shift against the strain on your good eye, it becomes a blob, then a sea creature, so you close your eyes to think of what's inside. Make the tour of the sailboat.

Last time you were there it was dawn. You left in the dinghy, left the bastard sprawled out in his bed, the sheets and his drunk flesh pouring into the small cabin. All drunk and dressed up. But now it is empty. In blackness you roam the cabin. You can feel yourself right there, opening the cupboards and cracking a bottle of fizzy water. Your narrow bed with the silk sheets and your clothes stuffed in the drawers. Your magazines and your watch in the cubby by the bed. It would be so easy to swim out there and sleep

22

in your bed and put on your watch. Can you steal the time back again for good?

Fuck these shoes, fuck invisible. Fuck these shoes. You kick them off and head straight for the shoes you now see before you, your own expensive sandals in the closet of the cabin next to the fire extinguisher. You're still an excellent swimmer even if you are getting old. You find you are running, the water isn't even cold or threatening, it is a pathway back; it will only take you half an hour to get there if you swim fast.

///

As you swim, the pulse of the dolphin's strange skin stays with you, like body recall that lasts long after the lover is gone. You feel sure that the dolphin embedded its sound-less whine in you and that now you too are a reader of the dark channels. Your body has vibrational power, it sends ciphers out behind each kick as if to say, Here I come. No fear of sharks or jellies – you'll sense them if they're near – nor of the airless darkness. Yes, in the water you are lightness itself, your fat flies off you, drifts away behind you, makes you lithe and sleek and fast. Queen of the breaststroke, you drop deeper underwater and you feel your old power come back. Warm and confident, you continue making wide arcs in front of you, leaving a solid wake behind you. You have a destination. A plan.

To forget the land. And the palms and the Precinct and the friends' villas you'd had visions of sneaking into. It is the sailboats that are sanctuaries. Their locks are feeble and, anyhow, you know where the spare keys are. You can picture them hanging from a tiny plastic buoy hidden behind the wooden shutters of the cabin doors or lying at the base of a heavy coil of rope.

The sea goes suddenly cold. Salt shores up and flocks densely around you, blindly magnetized to your skin. Because you are not the sea. You are blaring and human and soluble. You swallow a mouthful of the saltwater to feel the purity of its threat: how it is capable of dissolving your organs, then your bones, then lastly, your skin. From the inside out you will be nullified. You will become a suspension.

Liquid dust, you are nothing without him. You say his name out loud. Instead of saying "the bastard" you say his real name. Then you say it again, wanting to exorcise yourself of him, but the effect is opposite. His name overwhelms and belittles you. You cry out an embarrassed, stilted sound, barely any voice left. There is a shuttling wall of fire welling up in you, running slow and liquid, starting at your heart and spreading outwards. You push against it. The onslaught is almost peaceful. The enormity of murder being so straightforward.

Fucking bastard: the shark pit was a joke. Your joke even; you told the bastard and the others about it, that ten to twelve sharks slummed regularly at the foot of the Lowlands cliff. But it was a myth. So how was it that the bastard made a real shark appear?

You sob, right there in the middle of the sea. Your arms get drained of all their power, they hang disembodied at your sides. You have to stop, turn onto your back. Float. Your miracle and your plans evaporate: he betrayed you. He cut you out.

Tread water, keep afloat, breathe hard. Breathe so the red-and-white boat looming out in front of you comes to within an arm's reach.

The ladder is down. You bring yourself close to it and put your foot on the slippery step, feeling the hard tug of the ocean as you pull yourself up. You take your clothes off immediately, balling them up and pitching them overboard. Naked and dripping you watch them sink. But do they? You don't stick around to find out. Check later, you think. Your footprints will be dry soon. You'll leave no traces. Trust he won't remember what was there and what wasn't. You'll eat sparingly.

You take the key from the hiding place and open the lock without having to force it. As you crouch down the narrow stairs into the low cabin compartment, the smell of your own perfume hits you hard, as does your sudden

25

sense of house-possession. The familiarity and comfort of it all and how it's all still your world. The bastard's bed, everything as you pictured it to be: bottles and glasses spread out over the cabin, your watch, exactly where you remembered it to be, the food you'd thought of still there on the shelves. You take the food, fall into your bed, and eat it, doing everything all at the same time, making crumbs, putting on your watch, wanting to do everything, to have everything, to be everything this represents.

Jumping up again. Stopping yourself from cleaning up, but doing it mentally. Then stopping that impulse. You must memorize the arrangement of everything and not touch too much. Can fingerprints be dated? Will he expect to find that rotting tray of hors d'oeuvres next time he comes, or can you throw it away? It smells. Stop it. Let it reek.

"Rot on him," you say, food falling out of your mouth.

Curl your body up into your sheets away from the filth and into the darkness. You breathe in the smell of yourself. So pungent and new. Still you. Just deeper somehow.

///

By morning, it rains. Without thinking of anything, certainly not danger, you stretch out your arms behind your head and glance down to your thighs. A thing you do every morning with mild disgust and no definite plans to do anything about it. Then the usual thoughts of coffee and breakfast and cigarettes. Jesus, you say, through a cough and a laugh, your hands scramble around the cubbies by your bed. Where are your cigarettes? While your hands search, a hint of fear passes into your heart. Your hands continue searching while you look out your porthole window, scanning for something coming your way. Nothing: only more and more ocean water in one direction, and across the way, through the other porthole: the shore, houses, people as specks starting to fill up the beach. You pull your sheets up around you as you spot a pack of cigarillos under the bastard's bed. You make the effort to reach for them and light up with the bastard's gold lighter.

"The pit was a myth and somehow a real shark appeared to eat me all up. You piece of shit," you say, smoking. "You retarded piece of shit, feeding me to a myth," you say, getting louder, until you find you are raving and ashing all over the cabin, not caring about the glasses you smash on purpose, overturning the objects not nailed down to the floor. You run over to the bastard's bed, and rip the sheets off and rub the stub of cigar and all the ash and peels into his pillow.

"You piece of betraying fuck!" And you march naked and sweaty over to the fridge and take out all the food:

bright pink pâté, a sausage peeled back from its white covering, murky pickles, and make a pile on the bastard's bed where you eat it like you're actually a sow, or some kind of animal ripping the food apart with your chipped nails, letting it all smear across your face and drip onto your exposed rolls. You make stains on the sheets. You indulge in rubbing it in.

Eat until you think you must be full. Though you don't feel it, your raw, empty heart racing is the only sensation. Brushing yourself off, you go up on deck, smoking another cigarette to have a proper look at who or what might be looking for you.

Day two dead

(In which rain rises up from the ocean and
washes the rage away.)

COCKSURE, RADIATING FILTH. Tobacco on your nostril out-breaths. After a flash rainfall, as you lie on the deck with eyes closed, heat bears down on you through a crack in the clouds. You stay that way, leaned up against the front cabin window where you'd always sit with your 11 a.m. cocktail, and you revel in the post-tantrum energy. Of it being over now. The familiar aftermath qualities of thrill: of having won the argument and wrecked the house. Smashing expensive things just makes the point that everything is worthless to you anyway. Replaceable. Exchangeable. Except you won't let yourself be: you'll remake, reframe, get back to your beautiful self. Polish, style, adorn. Pull out your reliable charms.

In time, you smell smeared pâté cooking on your skin. It dawns on you, and you smile: the sun is sending you a message. You bake, you swell. You imagine this sun pouring life into you. How it is meant just for you. How it is telling you: you don't need to be dead. That you were subject to a miracle. Of always having received.

You picture the heel of your stiletto pushing the accelerator of your SAAB as you speed past the black boys on bikes to get to the Plaza Cavalia, the plaza at the centre of town, so much shinier than the real one in Italy. Then you picture the wad of clothes you arrived in slowly sinking to the bottom of the ocean. They hit the plankton soundlessly. You run your hands over your sweating naked body. It's on the fat side, sure, but your Bunny is still there pushing through the surface. Look how strong you are, how you swam all the way here. Look how your boobs are holding up. You don't look, you don't need to; you've memorized them from every angle in your bendy mirror room. Dammit if you don't see that Italian bedroom set again. No. Stop that Bunny. Make it new. Here you are, on the deck of your own sailboat, getting an all-over tan, pointing your breasts as close to the sun as possible. Hours like that, soaking in pretentious thoughts to keep other thoughts out, until the sky is nothing but a pane of glory pouring more and more of the island's richness onto you.

Anything, everything is still possible.

Then a second short rainfall breaks your tanning session and dampens your crystal message. Maybe you should hide out a little longer, find out what the bastard knows so far and what his next move might be. Figure out how to work your way back into the circle slowly. Do you come back entirely as yourself, or reinvented? Undecided, you do nothing much all day. You go back inside, tiptoe through the shards of glass, and plunk yourself back into the bastard's bed, in front of the TV with a bag of chips. From time to time you scan the cabin and notice you've done little more than piled new chaos onto the old. It is totally unrecognizable. You fall asleep feeling dolphin-worthy, safe at sea, voluptuous and exhausted.

Day three dead

(In which Her drifts away on a ribbon of Scotch tape and Bunny makes a plan.)

DRUGGED HAZE UPON WAKING. You wade through it. First the sluggish smell of fish as they meander through the shallow waters, then this unsteady view of the horizon going up and down through a crack of door. Finally the memory that, in the night, you got hold of the bastard's sleeping pills.

The sailboat bobs softly in the water and you bring

yourself onto your knees, fumbling as best you can through the broken glass and blankets that clutter the two beds; you rush from one side to the other looking through the portholes to search for someone searching for you. Could he already be inside? You jump to your feet to lock the door, and careen, off-balance. You smell the sharpness of cheap plastic having been snapped. Your body heaves like a stump of wood or something oversized that is at odds with the economical shapes and angles of the cabin space, and your numb limbs become some thick, dumb island that thuds to the floor. Your dolphin-Bunny power narrows itself to a shard, like the chip of glass you come eye to eye with as you lie there, the room now spinning out of sync with the dip and rise of the boat. You feel ill. You puke. And the reality of the stifling cabin, with all its new putrid smells of rot and smash-up, makes way for a fresh wave of paranoia.

Sticky and bloodied, prepared for deception, you stand, only to grab at furniture that rolls away on creaking metal wheels. The sea might be a trap, you think. There are so many ways the bastard could surround you. You think of how the food will run out. How flimsy the locks are. How they'd burn down your boat before you could lock them out.

Being burnt alive. Smashed to death against the cliff rocks. Devoured by sharks. Why glorify yourself when you know full well that if they find you now they'll simply shoot you dead?

Your brief handhold on a cabinet ledge sends your hip pivoting into an invisible, painful corner of something you miss seeing. Thankfully, somehow, you coincide with the bed, which you fall headlong into. You lie there breathing. You feel your blood soaking into the sheets. Rest now, and heal, Bunny. Nothing suspicious has been seen or heard today. "Pills, wear off, please, oh please," you implore to yourself. What you need are ointments, some fizzy drink, and a clear head to think this through with.

But you sleep again. From some other lifetime you are sent a sensation. You dream: of weapons that are dusty, dripping red. There are horses. Your soldiers following earshot away. There is fierce inhuman growling. The sound of galloping, yes, you are riding through a northern climate at dawn. So far from the ocean. Your ride is on land, the hard, frosted kind with trees as bare and grey as your hands gripping the coarse mane as you move at ruinous speed. A battle scream breaks the still air. Axes fall thudding to ground. A woman, not you, cuts a line in front of you, she runs across the icy landscape in bare feet, in a white dress covered in a cross of blood. You know you have murdered her, that you can do it, that you did do it, that you are capable and ready for anything bloodthirsty raw.

Jeez, what kind of pagan shit was that? You sit up and feel clear. Your eye, an exploded range of yellows and deep blues, with an etched black opening that inspects your face with measured care, concludes the cuts aren't that bad at all. Compared to your dream, at least. You dab at them with outdated Polysporin.

In a drawer under the bed, your hand pushes past a sequined T-shirt and a tangle of pearls to find a one-piece Speedo bathing suit. You squeeze into it, stretching the elastic with your rolls. It's something you've never worn but have had in there forever. Once a bikini-only lady, how easily you stuff your mouth now, cramming in what-ever food is at hand. You Band-Aid your cuts, then wind them and the rest of yourself in a sterile, waterproof tape, smoking a cigarette all the while. You put the pack with the lighter into a Ziploc bag, which you also tape to your back, crisscrossing your chest over and over, turning your body into one big holster to which you add Ziplocs of a small bottle of water, the pearls (why not?), some cash, and the only personal ID you find on-board: your NAUI Diver's Certification card. You can't quite rid yourself of this final proof that you are you. You giggle at the thought of yourself in that bikini you tossed aside, with your hair in its characteristic giant blonde poof hovering over your melon-perfect tits. All tied up now, you raise your arms up and down, stretch from side to side to test how well

36

you stay in place, how those selfsame tits hold firm, feeling satisfied that nothing rips. You leap thunderously onto the step to avoid broken glass, then go up on deck and take one last look at the cabin disaster. Will the bastard connect this mess with you or his own debauchery?

You decide: he'll connect it to you. You who are supposed to be dead and mangled by sharks. Fucking bastard. So you go back down, pull on a pair of his cowboy boots and sweep all the glass and medical garbage and crumbs and change the sheets, and then stand back to survey the twin beds glowing in their satiny gold like two bar tops. His eyes will gravitate towards that tidiness, and remember. So you rip the covers off to look at the effect. Too much of a prison-scene fuck-you absence. He'll know. You remember that your bed was made, and his wasn't, so you redo the gold and tuck it all in, look one very last time and decide on a dozen other small shifts, this way and that, before everything looks just like any other drunken night spent on board by the bastard alone. Or with her.

Her. Banish that, Bunny, don't think of Her, don't formulate her face in your mind. You've never seen Her, but you've pictured Her endlessly and right now you can't let yourself fall apart from the quivering, perfect form that becomes her image. Instead, let the abstract, acidic awareness of Her curdle upward inside you. Ask instead the question, the question that is uniquely about the two of you, you and the bastard, about your love and devotion: why, after all these years of knowing each others' every move, why hasn't he sensed you might have lived? That you do live. Why hasn't he come back? Just to see?

Night now, in a peculiar splendour of Speedo and tape, you jump over the edge of your sailboat with a loud splash.

The water is dark and fresh, and the ribbons of tape descend with you in a shimmery flutter that rises again quickly and surrounds you. But the salt stings. Skin flaps up on several cuts freed from your twining efforts. You relish the smallness of those pains against the security of the other objects which stay put, as you start the generous pull of your strokes.

Your plan, clear and simple: to swim from empty sailboat to empty sailboat, to spend as many nights as you need until the real plan of how to live again on your island presents itself to you. You are sure it will.

The NAUI card: your weak link. You feel it scraping at your back now every time you move. Yet, you can't tear it off. It's the symbol you cannot let go of for fear that the bastard has already decided to erase every living trace of you.

Can a person be entirely erased?

The thief's dilemma. Or the migrant's. You have been

38

a criminal, but you don't deserve such definitive, all-out exile.

And as you fall into a mute rhythm with the water, the only urgent goal is: swim as long as you can. The sea and salt will rub away who you are, leaving only the Bunny interior. That's all that will matter.

Scan the yellow lights each time you come up for air, and estimate the distances between the village lights and the shore lights, which are much closer, and then those of boats that spread out around you. But it's the boats that hide out, those without lights, the invisible ones that you need to bump up against, to climb aboard and disappear into.

Keep swimming. Feel as if by sonar: the circumference of the island, its salient boundaries: the tourist shores, the family-land beaches, the lowlands as they lead to the cliff where you got pushed. These are lesser known compared to the insides of the island, the hot, slick highways and main roads you've driven in your SAAB a hundred times over. The picture of yourself in your giant sunglasses, waving to acquaintances, is washed away, replaced by the image of your body become mammalian, shorn and buoyant, all pores reading every swish and shift of current.

Then a light on your left and voices, and you slink down low in the water. You float closer. Several people are on the deck of a white boat, clinking glasses, eating from a tray that flashes silver and smells of rich, ornamental food. You bow as low as possible into the water and pull in to touch the hull of the boat. You tread so gently there to listen, for ages it seems, but you don't hear a single word about you or your disappearance. Has the news not yet broke? Your shrivelled fingertips caress the fibreglass. Is that caviar? You are tempted to whisper to the man you sense is up there, just a few feet above you – Hey, I'm down here – and in your weakness, in that second, you imagine him hoisting your hefty body with all its baggy tape and Ziplocs up onto their pristine deck where you once belonged.

Thinking something is bubbling beside you, you notice the pearls have escaped their bag, they unfurl at your side like a jellyfish arm ballooning into a sudden whiteness. Then they are gone. You don't grab after them.

Instead you drift away from the sounds of their champagne, and the beach behind you recedes even further. You go underwater and enter a kind of sea-quiet state that blots out your cold body and your two bloated raisin hands until you come up against a wall that is dark like an impenetrable sky: too black to make sense of. Disoriented, not until the surface of the boat is at your nose do you realize that this hard, flat expanse is not part of the dark sea, or dark sky, but of Coke-Bottle's boat. And another party in full swing on deck.

///

On the water, sounds and space get all mixed up. Whispers that belong on one shore are turned to roars on an alien shore. In the late afternoon when the sun is at its zenith, sights appear across a span of water as if all has been turned upside down. Like the Fata Morgana mirages. You remember how this phenomenon once brought all the passengers onto the cruise ship's penthouse decks (where you Playboyed it, dealing cards by night, and drinks by day). They'd raced to the prow, confusing the mirage with a sighting of land or a mountain that was just there, out on the horizon. They'd put their hands out to touch it. And marvelled for hours, while you pushed through them, shivering in your summer tux, carrying trays of Chardonnay and bottles of Crown Royal. Even then you'd never forget a face or a tab. Your brain kept everything tidy, catalogued.

Now these sea anomalies count you among them, placing you at the vortex of a series of strange forces: distant voices sounding like they are right there beside you, dolphins emerging to save you. Your life becomes a mermaid's.

Stories of disappearances and balls of fire appearing in the night air conflate in your mind with the sudden appearance of Coke-Bottle's vessel. It has always been parked not five metres from your own. Which means somehow you've been swimming for hours in circles, not towards the foreign vessels parked in the bayside, but blindly paddling back again to the sailboats of your gang. In this there seems to be order to the universe, even if mysterious, and you sigh with relief.

Did your head make a thud against the hull? You aren't sure. You will your dolphin-miracle to extend into the present: more and more, invisibility has become your armour. The gang must be too drunk to have seen you swimming along, and now you can silently ambush them. You bring yourself close to the descent of the black hull, cradling its curve, feel it sucking you under along its slippery surface. Coke-Bottle, right there out of uniform, holding a glass, telling a story to . . . Who is that? From this angle, you can't tell. Goddammit if you'll be caught out wearing this luggage and all shrunk up to look two decades older than you deserve! You've always lied so successfully about your age. No, this time you'll hang back and observe them, see what they know.

Out of habit, you run one bloated, piggy finger under each eye to wipe away smeared mascara. Then you remember you haven't had makeup on in days. Jeez, they'd likely not even recognize you. Their drunken laughter infuriates you and fuels the growing temptation to pull yourself up onto their ladder and unveil your dead self to them. Like the Ghost of Christmas Past. The really fucking frightening one. And scream at them. The bastard would fall over dead. Oh, no question he is there. And even as you think this, you hear his throaty cough. The sound makes you instantly picture his bald spot showing when he throws his head over his knees in the glee of his own horsey laughter. Just days after having killed you, the über-bastard.

Do you really have to hang tight? If you are dead then you should be able to do as you like. But the fucking trouble of it is your shivering, halted breath, your flesh getting heavier, a blank slab – all proof that you are in fact here, though thoroughly exhausted. The weakness of just barely hanging on. Unable to let yourself drift closer to their voices, to hold on to the ladder for a bit. To rest your head on a rung. You hear the din of men and women, their self-entitled fervour so familiar you can almost imagine their clothes, their hands chunky with rings holding the rails, their flirtations that can lead to blows that can lead to that kind of late-night brotherly love involving guns and hard drugs and someone peripheral getting eliminated. You chuckle silently at your exaggeration. It mostly is. Except when it happened that one time and you shut your mouth, for him, forever. It was part of your love-deal. The exquisite promise of it shivers through you, alerting you to your humanness and how this body was once cradled warmly in his arms. For a second you believe his love could be refreshed, that he might remember.

Ready to give yourself up, ready to beg forgiveness and to be let back in . . . when a face appears, the black hole of a face draped by a falling blonde bob, so close you can smell the cloy of her perfume. It finds you and goes still. You will your ghostly shell to sink lower into the dark oil of the waters. She stays there wondering what to do because she is not seeing a stranger floating at the base of the ladder, she is seeing you.

She knows you, your white putty face. Only a woman knows the face of another woman without her makeup. What follows is the frozen impasse of neither one of you knowing what to do next. Holding your breath, it's like you are waiting for the high-pitched whistle to go off. But the hole, and what appears to you to be no more than a blonde wig floating against some celestial pattern of night sky, says nothing. Rather, you watch a red-tipped finger, attached to a disembodied white arm, point. The wig that turns away – you catch sight of its fullness, its lovely golden streaks, you recognize the stylist's work, you know the salon – swooshes back at you again, so that you understand she has checked the deck to ensure her discovery is hers alone. Then the black hole is sliced through with that white finger aimed at her lips. "Ssssshhh," you hear, ever so gently whispered. You glimpse the pursed red lips. Then as suddenly as she came, she is gone.

Your hand slips. The bastard's voice is booming in sync with several other voices, all responding to a splash not a metre from you.

"Did you think I wouldn't?" yells the Italian. You turn your head away from him, trying to become the very shape of the underside of the boat itself. He calls out again and you sense people leaning over the edge to jeer at him. You make out the sharp scent of the perfumed woman. Is she blocking you from their view? You're on the brink of identifying the exact label of the perfume when the swimmer calls out again. It's not the bastard beside you in the water, or Coke-Bottle, but some other guest who now begins a hard swim, full of splashes, making his way back to the ladder. As his enormous hands grasp at the bottom rung, your hand falls away, as if two hands having nothing to do with one an other just miss a fateful meeting. Your hand goes slowly, so slowly, down, not to arouse any attention. You let all of yourself go under, gently fluttering your body away from the undercurrent made by the man who jumped. You pray he won't retain some flash-memory of that hand.

Moving away, raising your ear out of the water, you hear the jumper hauled back up, followed by a wet slap of approval on his back. You make your way around the boat to where fewer Christmas lights dangle away from the mast. The quieter side of the boat. And there is the parked dinghy, to hang on to. Just barely able to. To get up into unseen. You squeeze yourself into the square stern, folding yourself as best you can under the bench, pulling the tarp overtop of you with the very last of your energy. You sink into the pocket of warm air made by your breath. Eventually the soft sound of your breath fills the space and coils around your body in comforting wafts. You have never felt so chilled in the Caribbean. Or so trapped. Or so lost. Or so free.

Day four dead

(In which Bunny becomes a stowaway on a superyacht)

HOURS LATER, when you've dried off and slept – it must be 4 a.m. – a couple stumbles into the dinghy. The man is singing absentmindedly. The boat goes topsy-turvy when he gets in, he is laughing, she is silent. Of course it's her: the one. That perfume. The woman with the black hole for a face, who peered down at you, who decided it was okay for you to stay invisible. You don't move despite her bottom's weight pressing onto the bench where you huddle. Her navy-and-white leather pumps. You saw them a week ago, half-price at the plaza. At least she doesn't shop in Miami. You feel a tenderness for these plump calves and swollen feet that bulge around the opening of the shoe.

How this acquaintance, whose face you cannot place, might be your ally.

"Jablonsky," sings the man, "are you there? Not like you to be this qui-et." He emphasizes each syllable, like he is seducing everything, the woman and the water. He ignores her when she doesn't answer. He hums and continues to row against the light, dawn-coloured waves. "I suppose you'll want to go back to the house now instead?" You sense that he is looking right at her. Which means, inadvertently, looking right at you.

"The boat is fine," she answers. You know her by her voice and her accent. She is the Frenchwoman with the Polish name who works real estate. More a friend to Coke-Bottle than a friend to you and the bastard. Nondescript and nice, a standoffish saleswoman who stood in stark contrast to the other island agents. Vultures, all of them, except maybe for her. You figured her to be independently wealthy, too refined for you and your gang. She wore understated, well-cut clothes, and yet never scoffed at all the bling and island flash. You had barely noticed her really, preferring the company of the gang of men who ruled this tiny empire of villas.

Now you wish, more than anything, to reach out to her, to whisper to her that you are there. She's on your side, not theirs. Instead, you let the boat rock you a little longer.

///

Their boat is a private cruise ship, a superyacht, run by a crew of eight. Two of the crew, appearing sleepy-eyed in white T-shirts, buff and twenty-something, usher in the dinghy and extend a hand to the shaky Jablonsky. Oh god, this is it. I have nothing to bribe them with once they pull back the tarp. You debate whether the NAUI card with your name on it is an asset or a liability. Will it be better to be known or unknown?

Jablonsky stays put.

"Leave me be for a moment, will you? I'm a little drunk still, not ready to come in." She laughs a deep-throat kind of laugh that you would kill to have imitated in your Playboy days.

What's going on, Jablonsky? you ask without a word. Give me a sign. What am I supposed to do here? And you listen to Jablonsky in the delightful process of smoking a cigarette at dawn. You imagine her running through private thoughts about what she saw that night as she quietly peered over the sailboat edge, having no idea that now she is partially crushing you, her stowaway. She kicks the tarp out of her way when she's done smoking, sending its hard edges ruffling up against your skin. You almost grab her leg, you feel violent towards her now. We had a deal babe! But as she steps out of the boat with ease, you realize the deal was all in your head, and you're back to square one, and the deck boys will be coming any minute to pull this vessel into the tender launch: the foldaway garage of this small ship.

You shimmy yourself out, making way too much noise. Then you stand, shaking all over, and sit back down on the bench. Then stand again and fall over, and catch yourself as the boat tips and you throw your leg back to the other side to make things even again, just in time. If you can hide out here you'll have access to food, clothes, a phone. Just make your stiff body do what it's told. Pull on the rope to draw your dinghy in to the side of the cruiser.

On board the sleek white lower deck you experience the familiarity of luxury. You let yourself fall into the hard, plastic angles, a kind of scramble and clutch that places you firmly on board. You face the bristling white emery surface, the ship's jaw edge. You exhale and moan. And feel your cheek flab press deeply into the grains, like you'd give up your entire weight into this one cheek if you could just stay there and get discovered. Be served a

50

filet mignon with a side of blue cheese and be put to bed by the stewardess. But you are running now, stepping up onto the main deck and moving along the narrow ledge past the design-improved porthole windows of the crew rooms. They could be anywhere, this crew. You want to get gorgeous again, before anything else. It might happen with Jablonsky and her king.

You feel shifts underfoot from plastic decking to plush, brown carpeting. The expanse of the main deck lays itself out before you: multiple rooms joined by loft-style partitions, mirrors of all sizes speckled with gold, decorative cabinetry of dark wood. A bachelor's den at sea. Mirrors and screens reflect the spaces in confusing ways – advantageously, you see right away, as there will be many places to hide. This becomes immediately necessary as you hear voices coming from a joining room, a bathroom. The husband enters, wearing a robe, Jablonsky next, wearing nothing. You see her from the back. You tuck yourself into a closet to watch them through the crack. You slide yourself down on the carpet. You can smell yourself against this tobacco-on-new-car smell: you have serious anxiety B.O. and the kind of bad breath that comes from not having eaten in awhile.

They are getting ready to spend the day in bed.

The maid arrives with a tray full of food: carved fruits, eggs, and toast with melted butter on top. Starving, you almost declare yourself as they settle under their feather duvets, clean and fresh. They eat, and smoke cigarettes at the same time. The husband flicks on the TV. You hear a sports announcer and smell the pineapple juice that drips down Jablonsky's face and onto the bed. Her tapered fingers hold everything so precariously that it falls out of her hands. You merge with her as she sighs deeply, satisfied, breathing in time with her until she coughs, looks at her breasts, then brushes the crumbs from them daintily onto the ground. Soon after, they both fall asleep. You stand up, look both ways from the closet and walk soundlessly over to the bed, stub out husband's cigarette and turn the TV up a few notches louder. You down a glass of juice, followed by all the coffee, gathering as much pineapple and toast as you can and shuffle back into the closet. You regret having to listen to the game while you eat. You wonder if they'd notice if you went back for a cigarette and smoked it through the crack. You are in a good mood, feeling like some good can come of this now that you've been fed.

///

Jablonsky and her husband sleep all day, as do you, seated upright in their closet with your bum squished into their shoes. When you look through the crack, you see the food tray has been taken away from the side of their bed and been replaced by a new one full of stainless-steel covered plates. The TV has gone silent. The whole place is hushed and you sense it is evening. Urgency now, to get out of here before they wake, to find a bathroom and clean up. You move your body to a hovering position and push the door against the plush carpet. Then stand there ridiculous and uncertain for a moment, shuffling stiff-limbed here and there around the partitions, trying to de-cide which way to go. Your tapes trail, they are covered in fuzz and feathers from a stole or costume of Jablonsky's, it all hisses behind you, your NAUI card slapping at your spine as you find the stairs.

On the lower decks things become less luxurious, the gold and brown is replaced with standard white and blue plastic. You hear plates and cutlery placed on a gal-ley table. The crew is there about to eat supper. You slip into one of the small bedrooms: a narrow space with a slim bed, everything in place except for a white T-shirt crumpled on the floor.

In the bathroom you pummel the toilet with pee. You aim the stream to hit the front side of the bowl so it makes less noise, at the same time grabbing the dark, wet face cloth at the sink to scour your face. You taste the salt in your pores come to life. A strange, alkaline odour fills your nostrils as you drop the cloth and lower the toilet seat, pulling a small makeup kit from the back of the toilet into your chest. The shower floor, still wet and giving off steam, is so enticing, you want to get in there and blast yourself with scalding water, but you reject it instantly. Too noisy. Instead you look for scissors in the kit, hands shaky, not finding anything but a nail clipper, and with that you begin ripping and breaking the tapes that encircle your body. They've become stiff, knotted with strings and covered in crap from Jablonsky's closet-floor carpet. You only half unravel them, fraying the edges without actually managing to disentangle yourself. Drop that and move on. Panic chiselling away at you.

You prioritize: put on makeup, find clothes. You turn to the mirror for the first time, one hand in the makeup bag already feeling for the sequence of application: foundation, eyes, lips last. And you notice your favourite: British Red. Then what you see reflected back at you in the misty mirror turns your heart cold. Staying perfectly still, you start to cry.

You've transformed into everything a Playboy Bunny fears but strives to keep at bay. Wrinkles, pouches, white roots straight as an axe running up against your greasy blonde locks. Snot fills your system along with the flash flood of tears that pushes through you. "Christ!" you whisper as loud as you dare: not only have you slipped into the world of old women within a few days, but the cloth you just wiped your face with was covered in hair dye. "Old woman" and, on top of it, a clownish mask. Two precise lines run through the middle of each cheek where tears fall.

Once, in your girlfriend Denise, you saw how a Bunny had crossed over into that nebulous place where beauty of a saleable kind is lost forever. This odd shared thing: nobody likes to say they were a Bunny once they're old. Bunnies don't admit to what they once were. Because then ageing gets measured ruthlessly. So they all go invisible and change their names until you can't find them anymore.

You get up off the floor and brusquely wash the black dye off your face. Which is pointless. Dye is dye; the question is, how long will it last? You swat at the bloody tapes that slap at your legs but they just fly around and chafe more. You are enraged with the irritation of it. The itch. Your inability to calm down enough to hold tight to one and carefully nibble your way through it with the small jaw of the nail clipper. Centimetre by centimetre until, again, you give up. Set your shoulders square, firm your mouth and smear foundation over the lot. You work quickly until it turns your face sludge-colour. Then add more to make an alien complexion. Followed by shimmering white, green, and gold eyeshadows brushed in bold strokes over your un-punched eyelid. It's funny to you how the other fat, slitted eye matches the peacock eye. Twins, but sadly, one got all the looks. Both eyes are streaked by a waterfall of Pierrot tears. You dab here and there, and wind your hair, thick with salt, upwards on top of your head where it holds itself. As you are about to return to the punched eye, to approach it from another angle, you hear what is clearly the end of supper for the crew. You catch sight of yourself in the mirror: half-turned and listening, unrecognizable. But you've run out of time to feel sorry for yourself so you re-zip the makeup bag and slip out the door.

///

And yet, hasn't your body become more malleable and lithe? Able to go behind, around and under spaces, unseen? You feel like just another shadow. Your getaways are getting narrower but somehow you remain protected. Has the skin of the dolphin rubbed its myth onto you? Of kingliness, of resurrection? Of being able to be in two worlds at once? When you look in the mirror you see how the garish makeup makes you more crazy, more outsider. More inhuman. How quickly you get used to it, your new state, yet at the same time how quickly your future becomes less and less tangible. It gets away from you. It becomes difficult to see what drives you.

You crouch among the pipes and other metal things that make up the domain of the on-board engineer, not far from the crew rooms. You nestle yourself into a nest of rope. Young people are returning to their rooms and then going to each other's rooms. You hear games and groping and snores.

Sluggish heat blows off the blocks of metal, you are sweating, and the hums and inner workings of the cruiser reverberate through you, like you and the ship are some great, slow fever.

You doze off then wake to things roaring up for the night. Laughter and bottles cracking. Upstairs, Jablonsky and her husband must be awake now, ready to begin their party all over again. How posh that would feel, to shake off the hangover with an early evening cocktail in the bath. You think of the life you made with the bastard. How much you want it all back now. You had a deal, and both of you knew that the quality of the love wouldn't last, but that the game would sustain you both. And the money. By sharing one conscience you halved the guilt for what you did. Some nights in bed, you'd curled up together and the heat of your bodies erased everything, all the bad you'd ever done, and as this weight disappeared, as other possibilities looked like they might open up – that you would stop it all for good – your complicity was rekindled. Into the indulgent first sip of champagne, then the next glass, then, "Let's have another." Then, "Let's go out on Coke-Bottle's boat tonight, and stop at the Cavalia. All our friends will be there."

You squeeze your pained eyes together, feeling all kinds of new thicknesses and creases, the animal-hoof smell of old makeup.

You get up and head back towards deck. As you pass into the inside of the boat your foot hits plush. The husband is there in his bathrobe, standing at the threshold of the bedroom. His short grey hair is messy on his head. He blocks your way out, stretching his arms up and then throwing his body down to touch his toes, making a giant growling sound. As he comes up you step out and into the lamplight and just stand there. The husband's face is red and puffy. He rubs his eyes. He isn't sure but he also isn't afraid. You push out your tits and grind your feet firm into the lush carpet.

"What the . . . ?" He throws up his hands, turning his head in both directions as if looking for someone other than you. You cough loudly. Your head lowers just a hint but you avoid looking down at yourself. Then he smiles, puts his hands on his hips, squints at you, as if he is seeing against the limits of his own eyes. Satisfied at having come to some sort of conclusion finally, he shifts his weight from one leg to the other.

"How did you get on my boat?" he asks, easing back

onto a chair. Then laughs, as if the question were simply protocol. He calls out amicably to his wife. "Jablonsky?"

Do you stay, or take off? You think you hear the word "unbelievable" muttered under this breath. But he's amused. Your eyes lock, his with a taunting glint, and despite the threat of Jablonsky appearing at any moment, you slowly lower yourself to the floor. The tapes crunch around your bum. The polyester points of the rug tickle your skin. You know, from your Bunny days, that if you put yourself at his feet, so to speak, your chances to manipulate him later are better; that, for a man, a woman getting down lower than him, while holding his eyes, reminds him of the thrilling hint of a blow job. So you fall to your knees. His mouth opens a crack and you see he's caught his breath. He opens his legs an invisible hint and puts his hand towards your head but then doesn't touch you.

Instead, he puts his hands on either side of his head, runs his fingers through his hair. The nails are short and manicured. You stay still. Hold his eyes. This is your only chance. You are a taboo that he is still considering. He hasn't called the crew, no, just Jablonsky. Did she tell him about having seen you in the waters last night?

The carpet seems to give off its own heat, residue from the sunlit day. Now he is looking you up and down, his brow strained, furrowed with pleasure. You wonder if he won't chuckle soon at what you've gotten up to. You recognize him, but just barely; you wish you could remember his name so that you could begin to say something. He holds out his hand. Very suddenly. You don't know what to do. You don't think he means to do this. It's an unconscious impulse. In this small uncertain moment before Jablonsky comes, as the warmth of the night encloses the ship, you reach out one blackened, dirty arm toward him, just to test what another body from your world might do, if it would accept you again. Then you hear the shush of the carpet and the instep of Jablonsky coming near. Your arm lowers a little. He laughs again, his face snaps back to its husband-self, as if to say, I had you there for a second, didn't I? This form of betrayal is so familiar you wince.

"I thought so," Jablonsky says, and picks up your hand that is still hung there, rejected, and you bathe in the aura of her gardenia perfume. She is dressed in a suit and her hair is combed. She helps you up, leads you to a small eating table, ignores that you're still locked in the husband's unwavering gaze. The husband dismisses you by getting up and following her. His game with you is now over. When she turns, she says your name out loud. Her accent makes it feel foreign, and all you can do is try to grasp at her features now that they are not the black hole anymore, but a mixture of peach-coloured skin pockets and wrinkles, the good kind, and you feel confused when, in the next breath, she repeats this name, yours you suppose, ending with:

"You can't stay here." And pushes an envelope across the table. Money, you know instantly. And her voice. It was her. Both on the telephone that day on the lowlands, and then again, on the sailboat. You want to run to her. The room is electric, nothing is as it once was.

Her composure is unflinching in the face of the husband, who now, grinning wildly, leans back so you see his belly. You don't trust him. You return to the authority of Jablonsky's seriousness as the dead weight of the boat under you cruises vaguely in the direction of Miami.

"Money," she says. "And you'll have to get a new identity obviously. You know all about that, I'm sure." You place both hands on the paper packet, their filthiness against its pristine surface fascinating you. The shapely nails with all those chips – they betray the integrity of name that she had spoken out loud. They are swollen beyond recognition. You see how they are starting to shake as you fold one on top of the other, one on top of the other. A new identity, yes, you see now that that is possible.

"But I don't want to leave the island . . ." Your voice is out of practice. Jablonsky ignores what you say.

"In some remote parts of Florida. I know there are places you could go."

I don't want to leave, you think.

"What happened to your face, anyhow?" And you remember. Laugh loudly at the ridiculousness of it all. A betrayal so complete it isn't worthy of consideration. How she won't see that all of this is false and that you deserve to be where she sits now all pristine and pricked up? She says your name again, as if trying to placate something growing in you. And you feel your status waning and you want to shred these blasted nails and all this fucking impossible tape, and a great distance widens between you-as-Pierrot and you-as-this-old-name she keeps repeating, as if to ask:

"Are you really there somewhere underneath it all?"

Pretend to swim your way to Florida, you think, to a new life, but really just turn heel once out of sight and come back to your island with the cash.

"No fucking way, Jablonsky." It comes as a whisper. It may not have been words but just thoughts. You stand up, suddenly furious. You push the envelope back at her. The husband gets up. "Now, now," he says, putting his arms on you. At first it's an echo of that hand he held out to you like a lover or a friend, but then he is wrapping those short, meaty arms around you. You feel how they are covered in grey hair, there is a certain kind of pressure and anxiety in his touch and then you feel his hands try to touch your tits, furtively so Jablonsky won't notice.

You find your own hands under the angles of his arms and untangle yourself from his grasp, backing away.

"Take the money. Please just take it," says Jablonsky, and you take it from her. She has seen everything. She teeters in what you see are short pumps, half the heel buried.

"We cannot know you anymore. You know that." You turn to the husband one last time, you are still vulnerable to trusting a man who has taken advantage of you. To turning tricks to gain favours. He stands there flushed, arms benign at his side.

"Run away," he agrees, then says your name. And you can't stand the sound of that name because it won't let you inhabit its luxuries, so you turn heel, for real now, rushing out into the night where the hard white deck is empty, where a waxing moon lights a path on the ocean.

///

You find a way to lodge the money into your bathing suit. Then swim away, in which direction you have no idea. Just get away from them before you have to kill them for knowing you are alive. As if you could actually to that.

You make fierce breaststrokes, your name on Jablonsky's lips ringing in your ears. The new identity, the one that peach-coloured face seemed so sure was still possible, looms out there before you, in the direction of

Florida. But you know you are probably swimming the wrong way.

The island is small. No matter how far you swim out, just like before, you are led back to the original shore. Until you are ready to be fully cast out, you won't be.

Day five dead

*(In which Bunny has sex with the
young man.)*

YOU REACH SHORE and come up onto the beach, settle
yourself into the leafy grasses that grow alongside a line
of large rocks that spills out into the sea, smell dryness
against the indulgence of car and suntan oils, sickly sweet
mango juice and parched, laundered towels.

You scan left towards a bluish mountain lane hooded
by palms and acacia, wide enough for a car to drive up.
The villas on either side are like small pastel mints of yel-

low, green and pink, nestled into clusters of trees that rise up towards a smaller mountain whose top is lopped off. At the foot of the lane is a decorative wall and just below it a beach lined with low-rise hotel resorts: open-air cabins selling Ting soda and Presidente beer. There is plenty of wind that morning before the sun takes over and changes how you see everything. For this brief, in-between moment, all edges are crisp and tuned to the sound of a single bird, one perched for several seconds not a foot away from you. To the right is the sea. Way out in the distance a giant cruise ship goes by. Your eyes move gradually from sea back to shore, observing mast upon mast of anchored sailboats.

You lay back against the sand, looking up to the palm outspread above you. Something you've looked at a million times, but never really until now. A formidable arch guarding over ever-narrowing white rings that lead to a smooth, green interior bark. At the top, a mass of loose layers of brown peel that bunch up like a shriveled pineapple. The look of it makes you thirsty. And you itch.

You creep closer to the nearest resort and stretch out on one of the lawn chairs before the attendants start to arrive. You rush over to the free-standing showers to rinse your feet with the lower faucet, then briefly rinse your whole body and hair with the vast spray of cold water from the upper shower. You take only seconds to do this and don't really come clean. The risk is to be caught by an attendant, even once. They would recognize you forever afterwards. Before you leave you grab two large, striped towels from under a lawn chair.

Back at your huddling place near the rocks, you make your fingers into a comb to rip through your tangles, then arrange your hair into a stiff nest. Once and for all, you rip the tapes off your body, leaving red welts up and down your arms and legs, wincing in pain as you go. With one of the towels you make a sarong around your body, with the other you fashion a sort of turban around your head. Couldn't you look like you are simply a tourist, an early riser and one of the resort guests? You emerge from the rocks, towel-wrapped, holding the NAUI card and the cash tightly between your boobs.

A desire for the comforts and privileges of your former existence rushes back into you. The desire to be held by a man who objectifies you. To be seen as an icon of the sexualized, available woman. Isn't that what the bastard loved about you? How you knew just when enough was enough, how to extricate yourself when a man was done with you, when he needed his space, how to put yourself at the edge of the bedroom to get dressed again, just out of sight of his ritual smoke. Then give him room, let him be. Make sure that if he did glance your way, you showed him your sweeter angles. Now that the sex was done, your voluptuousness was a hostility he'd like to forget. He wanted innocence afterwards. Until next time. You could get anything from a man when his dick was hard, but after that, you were like a rabbit darting in and out of the game, watching him, waiting to see, not sure if you could believe what he promised.

Trips to the Cayman Islands. Gifts bought on shore. In exchange, you were careful to look like the women from island-boutique ads in glossy magazines, those women parading designer Euro wares that were so glaring in this island world, so exalted – Hermès at the neck of each woman, grotesque Hublots on the wrists of men overnighting from St. Barthes, Perrier Jouet, six bottles down, as usual, at table six.

He adored you, but it was on his terms. And you knew, at all times, that you were also replaceable. Later on he loved you for other reasons: you began to become his equal, to understand how to be his ally. And then he saw your potential to be too equal, to have the power to be his enemy.

"That's right, I figured out your world a little, didn't I? When your belly grew fat I took that as I sign that I could let things slide just a touch too. Cutting my primping to half-time, what else was there to do but try to be on your side? To get in on it. You didn't like that in the end, did you?"

"I love you like this," he'd said, stroking your track-panted leg on a weekend. Together you'd pour over the real-estate files, the bastard occasionally jumping up to rant and strut around the table full of maps, and you, ever-present audience to his chaotic utterances. What he didn't know was that you were taking notes. Over tumblers of scotch you sorted the touchable from untouchable lands, those that you could rule versus those owned for generations by the blacks. Shanty structures mostly, but in prime locations. Impenetrable for inexplicable reasons. In the family lands there was another order of ring leaders, but not the paper kind. A lack of papers, more like it. Buried or lost for decades.

"We'll get to those parts when we run out of these," he'd say pointing to the mountainous sea vistas where he held monopoly, his hands moving up from one side of the mountain to the other, then from the paper to your arms to pull you away from where you too were now plotting. Yeah, you loved each other back then. And later on you'd put on your gold, and arrange your hair to fit with his vision of a nymph: tumbling blonde folds draping over all the white folds of your dress. And as usual, the guests would arrive and you'd say mum about the lands. Let him be king. You were becoming more than his prize. You were his partner.

The sun is still just coming in. Your sense of self-entitlement vaguely revived in you, you have no trouble sidling by a lawn chair and stealing a lady's empty beach bag.

The most eager guests are now meandering down to the wading pool for a yoga session. Their voices shatter the air, a confidence that doesn't fit with the fragile, flabby skin they carry as they pad by. As the hip-hop blasts out into the morning air, you spy a guest, who like you, has come onto the beach part of the resort alone. She sits on a lawn chair several metres away. Her nice, even tan and brash, hot-pink lipstick betrays that she is likely not from too far away, maybe from another island. No northerner on holiday. You envy the clingy gold jersey of the dress, how it fits her rather ample body, making her look so good. You take note of the heavy Yves Saint Laurent sunglasses as she removes them, and folds them into the dress which she takes off, stashing it into her bag. You get up then, and pass her so that the sun turns you almost completely into a silhouette. You perceive that she has seen you only as a flash, and that she has determined that you are staff, and therefore black. Or that you are one of the roaming band of outworkers who glide, almost invisibly, from resort to resort, each with a small bag out of which endless treasures cascade, from plants to patterned fabrics to shells to holding your hand and painting your nails right there on the beach. Rarely anything is sold. Then the mass of it gets mysteriously coiled up again into a small bundle before they amble away to the next beach. As she passes you, making her way carelessly down to the water without looking back, you say with the expected accent:

"I know you lady, seen you before, you wan' an aloe vera massage later on, I give you a nice one . . ."

Maybe your voice trails off with one of her arms waving at you, but at first she hardly even notices you, except as a familiar silhouette passing by, one with whom she understands she can trust her belongings. You laugh and say, "Alright, alright, lady, later on. I see you later on." As you bend down over your tummy rolls you draw in a deep and luxurious sigh, tidying up her striped towel, which the wind has blown sideways off her lawn chair. You pick up her hat and pat it twice so it stays put on top of her striped towel. Then you pick up her bag with that gold dress and YSL glasses rolled up inside of it, place it into the stolen beach bag and sling it over your shoulder like it's your own. As if it were simply full of the aloe vera stalks you carry with you from beach to beach, looking for a white lady to give a massage to.

You wait until night. At a garbage depot you find a plate nearly full of food the dogs haven't smelled out yet. You eat some greasy rice and the good part of a chicken leg, at the same time putting on the gold dress. It's a light-knit Prada and fits snug. The problem now is, you

71

haven't got any shoes. But since food is in your belly this problem feels like something for later, even though your plan was to get moving to the main street by six. With one foot you kick about the overturned garbage at the side of the metal drum. Your fingers comb upwards into the mass of blonde, arms feeling light because you've lost weight. So many times in front of a mirror making this same twist at the back with a prominent bouffant at the front. You're doing it, eyes closed, when your foot hits a flip-flop. It's hot-pink and pretty dirty but you figure there must be a mate. There isn't. You find another set, one with the thong ripped out, but between the three you make a pair. Then you saunter slowly in the direction of the next resort.

If you yourself believe you have a reason to be some-where, no one will question you. Walk up to the bar, look straight ahead. Anyone who looks at you: hold their eyes and their eyes will meet your defiance and fold with a flicker. How predictable all this is. A glimpse to your hair and your figure now stuffed into the gold Lycra and they are instantly defeated. They see almost nothing else. You pray so.

The bar is at the far end of a pool, flickering under torchlights, candle-lined and curved to face the sea. Ca-sually you dip your hand into the stringent aqua waters of the pool and discreetly splash your face. Rub the crusts from your eyes and the red-hot sauce from the corners of your mouth.

Sit on the barstool next to him: a late-twenty-something man, the one you've sized up as having a wad of cash in his breast pocket. Order something, anything, and drink it down, and let the bartender buy you another. You count on the fact that it will be paid for. Here he is, noticing you from the beginning, oblivious to your reek. He is young, and you see from his clothes, clearly not from here.

What is the cut-off point for the complete loss of sex appeal? Up until now, good grooming and posture, an attitude supported by money and friends, all have done wonders to hold off age. Then one morning you wake up and you hardly recognize yourself anymore. You'd seen this happen to others, but you couldn't figure out how or when it would happen to you. It would happen. But not yet.

Your shoulder turned to the young man has the effect of drawing him closer to the bar ledge. He pushes his drink your way with his index finger. You laugh to give him a flash of your still-good teeth: over-white and capped, the artificial blinding kind that outshine lipstick, which you don't have anymore. Keep talking, you think, you are saying something sassy to the bartender, overdoing it, mesmerizing him. The bartender throws back his head and laughs. He leans in. Too close maybe, and you gracefully back away a little. Neither one of them can feel threatened by the other. Nor can they feel sure. Keep the laughs going and any unsavoury scents from blowing their way. The transaction itself is wry and scripted on both sides, but mostly with the intent to create tension so that the young man is torn between feeling slightly left out of this sexual game and desiring to step in, to play the game. He seems a little unsure. Bashful yet somehow bold. He wants to try. He wants to be a man. He doesn't want to fuck it up.

You sense all of this, and you sense your advantage without even having looked his way. Now his wrist with the thick watch rises towards the bartender who shoots an annoyed glance at him – the young man orders two drinks: one for himself and one for you. The bartender relinquishes, straightens his shoulders, and slips back into his aloof persona, pouring and sloshing martinis.

One hour later, in a villa not a kilometre from your own where the bastard surely is, you are frantic in the young man's renoed bathroom, armed with his razor. Breathe, breathe, you tell yourself. You made sure he kept the lights off, kissing him at the car, then again as you entered the doorway so he wouldn't find the light, so instead was searching blindly to put his hands all over your body. Which you also held at bay. Silently putting your flip-flops into his garbage bin, you entered a chilly, high-ceilinged house.

"Let me use your bathroom first," was all you'd said. He pointed through the darkness to a spiral staircase made of glass. You walked the first half of the ascent, then raced the second to the bathroom where you turned on the shower and scrubbed and washed your body and hair. "Hurry, hurry . . ." you now whisper to yourself, raking the razor over your armpits, up the sides of your vagina, along your calves, with a steady, practiced hand. Jump out and rub yourself dry, comb your hair, ransack his drawers for face cream or anything resembling makeup. All you find is a jar of Clarins for men and a single black eyeliner which you figure was left by a fling. He doesn't seem to have a present girlfriend. Or even live here himself often. The bathroom is empty, like a hotel. You place the packet of money and your NAUI card next to the sink, intending to collect it later on. You come back down the stairs naked and burning hot in his long white bathrobe.

"A freshen up."

"I gathered." Which is cue for him to gather you in his arms. He luxuriates in your full bum, squeezing it and kneading it into circles. Slips his hand into the robe, lunges and bites so you have to laugh a little, slow him down. He is breathing fast, trying hard to do it right. To control himself. He pulls away shocked, eyes wide.

"Upstairs?"

"Let's just sit awhile."

"Here?"

"Sure. Anywhere is fine."

Sex with a young man when you're just "passing" for young. Not yet old. Something you do with pleasure, yet stand outside of to observe: a certain ravenousness brings you there quickly; reckless false moves he believes in, so you marvel; a violence you haven't felt in awhile and know you could only tolerate a handful of times. How long could this intensity last? So you smile and stay with him. Love is always getting mixed up with lust at his age. You think: tenderness and an endless hard cock. So you do it twice.

Afterwards, while you had your eyes closed to dream yourself out of the hell and back into the cool caressing smell of marble, freshly cut, he got dressed again. It wasn't perfect and he knows it, and you don't care. He offers you a drink and you open your eyes, see the flash of his skin that matches the amber liquid he's putting into your hand. As he plunks onto the other end of the couch, a hot night breeze drifts in over you both.

Ice tinkling in the oily amber liquid when you're dying of thirst. Suck the cubes and he brings his face close to yours: a narrow nose and eyes that see you but also seem to be looking right through you, or far off to some other distant purpose. You guess Dutch because of his name and accent, when he says, "I'm Flemish. That, and . . . other things before." You feel your eyes narrow, trying to sort through what he can mean against your own prejudices: his skin colour is so distinctly from the island. He looks like he'd be the brother to all those young girls who walk around with older white men, driving their cars, toting their babies. And then the very word Flemish: something antiquated in your mind. He is from here but also has those northern traits: dark circles under the eyes and a refined, narrow nose. Like in those paintings you saw once in a book on Coke-Bottle's coffee table. But this young man has nothing to do with all that red drapery and those high foreheads. And yet, you know his sense of home is divided somehow.

He brushes his hands over your legs. "And these?" The welts are brilliant red and have been brought to life again by the shower and the sex. Now that he's had you, he eases back onto his own couch. You see he is fascinated, but underlying this is an arrogance that, no matter what, will make your time in his life temporary.

"I'm new to the island too."

"You are?" You nod, as he looks you up and down examining your parts, one by one, to distill you down to something he can understand.

Deflect his calculations by holding his eyes to yours.

That way men have of assessing you both for your beauty-value and your use-value. As if they are torn between the two. Cunning, but there is something else, some underlying motive that drives him. You lay back and run your hands through your hair. You're so tired, you realize, and wish you could just fall asleep right here in his enormous white couch. Letting your eyes close again, dozing, you feel the taut rungs of his breast and shoulder bones brush past you. The sound of the tap, then a little while later a kettle boiling. And his voice, suddenly animated and loud:

"I've been invited by the local baron it seems. To a party." He laughs and looks to you questioningly. You say nothing. "He accosted me yesterday in a café, I have no idea how he knew who I was. Anyway, I'd love it if I went with someone. I like that you're not from here either."

Your eyes flash wide. Heart flickering in two directions at once. The use of that word 'baron' said like a joke can only mean one thing: the bastard. The bastard's having a party just as he always would for a newcomer. Your innards writhe at the fact that his life hasn't changed despite having so recently murdered you. But this feeling is calmed by the remote thrill of this young man wanting to see you again.

Best to say nothing, even though you are dying to ask more. Half an hour passes, and why this mutual peace passes as though in love, you can't say. And you both seem to drift off, to tune-in to the blare of crickets and warm wind from the balcony. You sleep awhile, naked legs intertwined.

Then both of you at the door, a little shell-shocked, teetering on your feet over the queerness of standing next to each other, not sure now where your intimacy stands.

He looks at your feet questioningly.

"Don't worry, I left them by the car." His brow furrows then smooths as you blow him a kiss.

That night you walk the long route back to the shore. Into the blackness you spot an abandoned sailboat, invisible but for another boat nearby spilling light onto it as it tips and totters on the waves. You ready yourself, disrobing. The gold dress fits fine wrapped around your head and you rush down the cold sands, naked, and stride into the warm waters. They invite you. Your strokes are powerful. You've eaten, drank, fucked, and have a plan: to accompany the young man to the bastard's party. It's then that you realize that with all the echo of his tongue still burning on your skin, you forgot your NAUI card and the packet of money in the young man's bathroom. Panic turns your heart for a second. Then as you go underwater, and stay below so long, you wonder if you still need to breathe to stay alive. You wonder what really matters anymore for your survival? The symbolic value of those objects vanishes, as below you, the ocean opens up like a consciousness, a galaxy of dimmed green flecks in which your heavy mammalian body becomes muscularly slow, almost dissolved. The envelope of money and the identity card have no currency here. Money and Bunny can't help you anymore, you think. Eons away, stars pulse like tiny bright minerals. You come up gasping for a giant breath of air, and you drift, breathing hard, your thighs brimming ovaline and spent against night sky, until your head gently bumps up against the boat. As you lay in the clean sailor's bed, the rock of the boat draws you into a calm, lucid sleep.

Day six dead

*(In which Bunny goes to the
family lands.)*

COOL AND OVERCAST. The main sail flutters. This boat is much like the rest but with some country-chic flair. You run your hands along the lacquered honey-brown panels. You push the ruffled floral cover off and go to eat whatever's in the fridge. A cold hotdog nearly gags you. You make up the bed, at the same time searching the drawers underneath for a swimsuit.

You find a Laura Ashley bikini, two sizes too small.

Busting out of the B cups, you wonder what to do with the gold dress you'd worn on your head for the swim. Pretty soon it's going to be like a relay of clothes left between sailboats. How funny if you were to return to a boat and find your original outfit, the one you wore over the cliff. Now, the options before you: dresses in mauve and dusty blue, with white bibs in the shape of triangles, diamonds, and circles. Over your dead body . . .

You wind the still-damp gold knit back around your head while eating a carrot, and rifle again through the drawers. The lady of the ship is clearly an Avon investor. You set the distinctive pink case on the bed and open each of its shiny black drawers, taking out some things. Then pat and mop your face, armpits, crotch, pulling aside the bikini bottom, and wash your vagina with a wet face cloth because you're within arm's reach of the sink. Looking in the mirror you apply baby-pink cream that is cold against your cheeks, then a layer of beige powder, followed by sand, pink, then turquoise eye shadow, forming a dramatic zigzag gradation right up to your eyebrows. Then thick mascara and liner. Gloss on the lips. You feel better now. Even the babyish bikini makes you look cute and it'll go with your curls. Maybe you'll even spend some hours tanning today.

But once in the water simple thoughts are replaced by a tranquil blankness. You swim with your head above the surface to protect the Avon. The waves lap calmly against your chin, warm and tingly. As you come near the shore, the scene unfolds before you in slow, lazy detail, mostly people arranging their towels for a day of lying down. The stillness of the palm trees and the solemn sunbathers on the beach steady you. All that sun being soaked into leaves and skin gives a meditative rhythm to your strokes, a tranced repetition, and a pall of sunlight, a nothingness, is cast over the ocean, blaring over the surrounding sand, so that your mind opens and strange thoughts enter. Scenes of yourself in perfect solitude, wandering stretches of the island invisibly, living contentedly off scraps, being fed by the town, the jungle, and the ocean, then more active visions of yourself carrying out quiet, calculated but absurd acts fueled by the feeling of injustice. Soft apocalypses blow up in your mind. You set random fires with the last flame of a found lighter, smash a lowland rock soundlessly through a car window. Shit on a doorstep at dawn. Or kinder acts that would be like rewards to strangers. You don't know why, but somebody would be given the gift of something stolen from the plaza boutiques; as you walk the warm concrete mains some man might be drawn aside, into the bushes, for a silent, expertly executed blow job. You see how your body could morph daily, how it could come closer in look and kind to the blinding brightness of the island, how it could transform by night into the dark sway of sultry bars bordered by the succulent morbidity of the mountain with all its foliage. Living outside of yourself and time. Adopting the clothes of others. Maybe even a mask, maybe made up of your own hair? Or stalks of dried leaves, fruit detritus, broken sunglasses, things plucked from the garbage, to make yourself truly unrecognizable. Tunnel-visioned, muscular and untouchable, something symbolic so you could wander more freely in your new Bunny power.

Somewhere in that reverie, the real scene comes up abruptly. The contrast smacks you when your foot hits the shallow point of sand and you stumble up onto the beach full of people. It is now, as your heavy thighs readjust to land and you drag your body forward, that you remember what it is you have to do:

Air dry, and march to town like you own the place. Those words sit unsteady in your mind as you step forward, the aloe ladies with their baskets passing you on their way to the resorts. Something in your walk, your eyes without sunglasses, makes you doubt you'll hold sway. You're not carrying a single thing in your hands. How will you buy hair dye with no money? How much time do you have left?

At the central square you sit by the edge of a café and watch the men in their fifties with young, exquisite girls on their arms. Beautiful girls, Russian dancers, you've seen them all before at cocktails and parties. At your own parties. They'd fawned over you, admired your good taste, what you said, what you didn't say. They were pregnant and growing silent. Driving their old boys' sports cars into town, finally secure. Finally they could breathe. You shake your head. Of course, of course, those girls aren't stupid.

You have no idea how long or how far you may have to walk in the coming days. Land now. It's harsher than the ocean. How it sits there, laid out under the sun for hours like that, with nothing to cool it off. You squeeze your eyes shut. Open them again onto the crisp scene of shoppers and drinkers and high-pitched music and movement in all directions. The lowlands, where you need to get to, are opposite to the town: dusty, rocky, lined with desolate roads. You'll walk like the maids do. From villa to villa, a plastic trough full of cleaning products in one hand, the other hand wiping your brow.

Which you do endlessly until you're sure there isn't a stitch of eye shadow left on your lids. Nothing happens. No one looks at you. No one notices you. Nobody recognizes you or calls out to you with a big smile on their face to buy you a drink, and nobody takes your arm in theirs and makes aimless small talk to maintain the circle of friendship. You're getting hungry. Screw those carrots, you should have eaten three hot dogs instead!

And you realize you've let the day get away and it's too late now to find a way to the lowlands. You're not prepared for that. You at least need a water bottle or a ride of some sort. You decide to walk in the other direction, the eastern part of the island is flatter. The names of the villages there are like saints.

Walking calms you. Gives you time to think about your past and your future. You don't want to dwell on the here and now, it's too wide open, too loose, there are no borders to cling to.

As you approach a village called Saint Francis you feel your step lightening, your body becoming airy. You go freely into places you wouldn't normally go. You go along walkways that are broken and overgrown, narrow green paths lined with random things: arrangements of driftwood, potted palms with cracks and dirt spilling out, geckos, dogs, faded clothing left behind. Your eyes are bright and alert, opened wide onto plots with fences painted red and turquoise. Looks your way are mixed: the men and women, sweeping walkways or busying about their properties, call out to you or say nothing. You've let your posture go a little. With your sweat and rumpled dress you feel you blend in. But of course you don't.

"Hey lady," one calls, casually.

Another looks at you as if it's curious that you are there. But not really. Not curious enough to stare.

Here you are clearly an outsider, since these are the family lands.

You keep walking. Children playing a game push past you. You've been ambling up a mountain road and haven't seen a car in ages, when one finally comes cranking and chugging along little faster than your walk. As it inches by, something about the passenger catches your eye. The shape of his head is familiar, you recognize the profile as he turns to the driver. He is laughing, speaking another language. You see now it is him: the young man. He doesn't recognize you. The car passes on by.

Where it heads it is much cooler. You are wandering the young man's way, not following him.

When something else catches your attention. A thin bright green snake goes steadily over the cracked mud of the road. Ordinary for it to be there, except that as you approach, the snake slows down, loiters at the base of tree, no longer hunting for a nest of lizards or mice, but rather stalling by curling this way and that without apparent purpose. When it finds a post from which to inspect you, you meet eyes. Then you are following the snake as it moves gracefully towards a dense area of palms, behind which are shadowed houses held in by a splay of pathways barely wide enough for a car.

///

Night catches up to you. You were daydreaming, sitting on a stump watching the hypnotic uniformity of the jungle, the slow turn from brilliant green to the colour of a hunt at dusk.

Yellow lamps light up in the small houses, and you hear footsteps, the sound of family members coming home for supper. Pots banging, the din of cooking, the talk of what happened that day. You feel the urge to listen and be part of it.

Without thinking you walk a path that leads straight to where the young man is. How you know it's him you have no idea, but sure enough you are leaning against the wooden slats of a house, out of view. You hear soothing music, then his distinctive voice. His outsider tone separates him and yet you sense he is more than welcome.

"So you've come back to claim your acres."

"I have."

"It's here for you, you know that. All you have to do is take it, choose it."

"I'm truly grateful, I am."

The sounds of smoking, someone rocking nearby with a baby.

"Always and forever these lands are just waiting here, for their family to come find them and build something. What will you build?"

Silence. You sense the young man leaning over.

"The land is foreign to me still."

"You were born here. Right here in this very house. That's why." Chuckling. "The house remembers you! It's called you back from your other place."

"Well that's where I live now. Where I have to stay."

"You'll see. You'll see. Tomorrow we'll go make the tour, find you a good house plot where you'll be happy and bring your wife to come back to."

Something in your heart plummets southward. His voice murmuring neither yes nor no.

You edge deftly away from your eavesdrop feeling mercurial, heavy and light at the same time. You retrace your steps through the tangle of roads until you come out to the main road. Compared to the cool darkness you came from, this feels like a highway. Your mind is heading beachward as if in a trance, ushered along by the hush of the jungle, and then the large S of the snake appears. As it moves, its rhythm becomes the buzzing shape taking form in your brain. Two perfect arcs intertwined. The life of the island and ... The snake snaps and you run full-out to the shore, throwing off your clothes and diving in.

As you skim along the surface of the black, choppy water, you look up to see you are surrounded by boats full of people. All the boats are busy tonight, lights on deck blazing, couples watching the stars, people yelling from one side to the other. You've come to assume that there would always be one boat available to you.

You are losing sight of your plan. You consider squatting on the young man's land once he leaves. Or, what? To squat on your own land?

Suddenly tired and deflated, you swim back to shore, to the gold dress you'd tossed on the sand. You shake out your hair and walk to the bar. When you arrive you make the best of yourself in a mirror. Come out, Bunny. The type of man you used to know is there.

Dark, slick, perfumed. Older. Tactless, with all signs of wealth encumbering his neck and wrists, his small balletic feet in Italian leather slip-on shoes. He is the spitting image of the bastard.

You amble his way, already holding his eyes, the room seems to have conspired to this, it is cosmic timing, you know before it happens that it will all work even though it shouldn't – you aren't actually his type – and nothing to lose, you arrive at his side:

"If there is anyone in this bar worth taking home, it's you, gorgeous."

He grins. And falls for it. So much so that he hasn't even glanced at your bare feet, nor at other things that designate you as slightly trash. Already his meaty hand is on your waist pulling you closer to him.

You chalk up your success to habit. The hunger to be liked, to be powerful, to be seen, is fading, but you stumble through the motions anyway, walking through a version of your past behaviour, some final vestige of the Bunny power. You have to do it one last time to prove it to yourself that it isn't the answer.

"I was just thinking of leaving."

You clamber along the pavement to his car, barely held up by his drunken clutch, and agree to go to his place. You whisper in his ear: the promise of other delights, your body at his disposal, your companionship for a night of drugs. All of the above if he wants. You feel mildly shocked that you haven't heard of him, or seen him before, but there are so many newcomers to the island, an influx you notice only once you're in the casinos or big restaurants.

Entering his mint villa, the man ignores you, setting himself directly at his glass dining table, clearing the magazines and papers with a brush of his arm. Backing away with the first glimmer of regret, you watch him from a distance, see him as a hunched-over helmet of shiny, black hair. You keep this circle of black with its thinning centre in view as you amble about his Deco-revival apartment. The single glass of wine in your system inspires you. The reawakening, the shivers the tinkle sounds give you: of diamonds, of crystal, of the sequins on dresses going by you at parties. In the bathroom, you place both hands firmly on the deep vermilion counter.

You turn your head from side to side in the bulb-lined mirror, seeing the echoes of your youthful beauty still just-there, when you hear the man call you.

"Bunny," he growls from the table. "Where have you gone?"

You pet the purple ceramic swan where a dry washcloth is resting. "Hey you, I have one just like you at home, but she's peachy peach." You cast one last look at the array of women's cosmetics, perfumes, and brushes, but now they have no appeal, they look dusty and bleak. Objects trapped in another time.

Then come back to where the man is at the table, slouching with legs wide, do a line of coke that he sets up for you on the hinge of his foldover, just above his pubic hair, his pooch – you grin at him as you inhale the sour waft that puffs out of his unbuckled pants. You do several more lines. Pulling away, with a flip of your hair and a sniff, you watch him as he eases back into his chair. He's busy tipping back his bourbon glass until all you see is his throat. You feel your neck grow long, you turn towards the alcove of a room far off in the house, you can see it there, some other deep shade of orange, the walls pixelated by serious mirrors lined up like swords. His arrogance, his open shirt which emits imported perfumery and sparse, unruly chest hair, his messy slaps on your ass – it is all familiar.

"Champagne is what we want!" he yells out, slapping the table. "Darling Bunny gorgeous, my new friend," he reaches out for you. Misses. Laughs. "Why don't you go get us a bottle and serve it up like you would have for the playboys?" he says as he takes another swig from his half-empty of bourbon, and gestures towards a dark hall. You grin at him, feeling detached but game. Barefoot you go, happy to be high and walking away from him. The cases of champagne are stacked in an empty room. They release a gentle clinking memory that streams up inside you: of too many bottles in the arms of the bastard as he'd enter the room yelling, "Tonight we celebrate!" Of endless supply. Easing one out of the stuffing brings on a surge of glory. Back you go to the table on tiptoes, pretending you're wearing the requisite three-inch Bunny heels. But he isn't there. You find the kitchen and open the bottle and place it on a tray with two flutes. You wander like that, still on tiptoes, balancing a tray of champagne on one hand, pretending to smoke with your other, when you hear a whistle. It's him. Upstairs it seems, ordering you to come.

"You're actually going to whistle for me? Jesus." Something new in you doesn't like this. But you play along because it's his game, ultimately, until you win him over. As you walk through the house, breathing in the crisp smell of wealth, the devil in you rises up again.

"Bunny's back," you whisper, pinging the flute of one of the glasses against the bay window that overlooks the sea. "Cheers." A meaningful sound of response: a barrage of nearby waves. You feel the pulse of the ocean pulling you towards that small opening in the window when a warm wet mist hits your face, creating a precise longing to be naked in those waters. But you tear yourself away. "Coming," you say softly, in no particular direction.

You enter the bedroom soundlessly and see your man laid out, face-up, on his giant round bed. A reddish glow from the mini chandelier augments the pinkness of his skin, the rise of hairless pouches and folds on his chest. He seems to have half-stripped down, resting one hand on his limp cock, then passed out.

You set down the tray on the lip of the divan (in the shape of real lips), pour yourself another glass, and stand there looking around at the room, ready now to approach him. You had looked forward to sleeping on a real bed, and forging new alliances, but now the man looks uncannily dead to you, and as you creep closer along the white carpet and let the tips of your nails graze his face near his mouth, you strain to feel for his shallow breath. It's barely there. The bubbly stings your throat as you take sip after sip, watching him like a hawk. Now you don't want him to wake.

You want to pour champagne all over him and his bed.

To straddle him with your heavy legs and bite his neck way too hard so he screams. To squeeze his hips with your thighs as a small trickle of blood stains the seam of his white shirt at the collar, to pull his head back by the measly hairs that crown the bald spot. You fucked me over, you bastard. Nails digging into his chest, making welts, his eyes snap open wide with surprise. It makes his cock hard to be dominated. But you slam your hand over his eyes, gripping and kneading the skin at his face the same way you do with your other hand on his cock. Don't move bastard. But he extends his arm, ever so slowly, afraid. "I see you bastard, whatcha doin'?" You allow his hand to drift over to the other side of the bed where it flips a switch that sends the bed into a roar of invisible electronics. The bed begins to turn like a parade float. You grin. Watch him bleed. Bend down and rub your face into the blood so it smears, so you can smell it. Come. Come get him. Even if I love him. Love him. Hate him. Want him. Hate him. Love him. You are whispering now, chanting. The rancid scent of his blood makes you want more. Makes you hungry. Your tongue is dripping with blood-striated saliva. Sparkly lights from the ocean penetrate the bedroom. You watch him dully, almost dead-eyed. Everything glistens now cool and wet with the saltwater pouring from both your bodies. The room is circling with dizzying speckled lights, then his cum is spurting

95

and with that you shake the champagne bottle, wasting it, screaming out a low-pitched moan.

At that moment his eyes open for real. They are so clear you think he must have been waiting there, quietly watching you the whole time. The champagne sizzles icily all over the bed. It lubricates your skin so you slither one thigh off of him. You want to get out of here, but now the man has reared up onto his hands. You watch streams of white rivulet to a V at his dick. He flips you over, pins you down, but you are too wired to be held by him, and without a thought, you rise to your knees, push your ass against his belly then bang the bottle against his head. The sound is dull and the bottle doesn't kill him.

"Oh, for Christ's sake . . . alright you bitch." And he falls back onto the bed, moaning gently, rubbing the thicker portions of his black hair over and over into a dark red mat, until he grabs the bottle himself and cracks it against the side of your face. The blood cascading from your temple, down the entire side of your body, only gives you strength. Not yet, bastard. And like an animal you back away on the bed, watching his every move until he goes still and you hear him snore and snort in fits.

Your first few steps – the blood has gone all the way down to your foot – leave mulish red prints until gradually, as you tiptoe back through the house, retracing your steps, they stamp sticky and random. On your way along the hall, there is a pastel room where you see a fresh bouquet. Red roses. And an open closet. Oh, yes, a woman lives here. Wanting to look, to take things – it occurs to you you should steal money at least, but that thought goes straight out of your head. Money hasn't been necessary or relevant to your survival. Still, you look through the closet. Fancy women's clothes, rows of extravagant heels. The wooden hangers crash as you swat through the dresses. Into a small bag you stuff something red and silk and toss in a pair of shoes. You wind a scarf around your head to staunch the blood still trickling from your temple.

Then you creep down the stairs. Dizzy and shivering on the outside, but on the inside, stealth and calm.

As you move fast and rhythmically to the door you aren't sure what it is you're running from or to. You hit the metal gate in front of the door with your entire body, expecting it to swing open, but it doesn't. It's locked from the inside.

You crumple, nearly faint against the door. And you picture that black metal key the man used when you came in, but you were kissing, eating his face, and blind in that moment.

Almost used to it now. Crawl spaces. Hiding out. Waiting for the right moment. But to maintain your focus, you need to be on the move. You need to get back into the water and swim, and for several moments you lose focus entirely as light-headedness feels restful against thoughts of being underwater. But you are trapped in this house. Its open, marbled hallways are claustrophobic. Static objects on the walls: a print of a stylized woman demurely looking out from under a hat, a ceramic shell that juts shiny and menacingly in mauve from the wall; the energy of the villa is blown out and glossy, cut off from the warmth of breezes outside. The hum of the air conditioner sends out radiating waves of depression through your body. You feel the hidden dust, the whiff of a rotten banana in the kitchen garbage, the tang of bubbly left over in your mouth. What was familiar and comforting is now eerily foreign. You are trapped. Need something to do. Thankfully a pack of cigarettes appears in your line of vision. You slump to the floor in the laundry room next to the front door and smoke so you can breathe again. And make a plan. However much you squeeze your eyes shut and beckon the swell of the ocean, nothing happens, you toss between wake and nausea and sleep. You pull damp towels over you to stay hidden and warm. You try to conjure the snake that led you safely to the young man's house, and again get nothing, no guiding image, until finally the girlfriend arrives home in the early hours of the morning. She is careless with the door and you exit without any fuss.

You slip out into the dawn with her things in the bag, running barefoot down Folly Road. The hedges are short and bright, they smell fresh compared to your skin. At the entranceways you see the maids just arrived, you see them bending and gathering. A woman with her dog looks straight into your eyes as you go by.

Day seven dead

(Bunny and Shark.)

THE FLASH OF TINTED WINDOWS, and a car rolls by. You put your turbaned head down and keep walking. Will you be seen? All the bad things that could happen to you race through your mind. For a second, out into the warm, open air, you can't see straight. Then you run a little, get your feet back, feel like you're getting somewhere. Fluttering above the deeper layers of fear are coke-infused images, delusions of grandeur so overwhelming your limbs start to expand, you feel whole feet taller. You feel like your skin is burning and electric. Your eyes sharp, they whip from street to rock face to car to bush, and finally all you see and all that drives you on are the contorted faces of three men: the bastard's mixed expression of agony as he threw you over, the young man grimacing with orgasm, the horrified mask of the last man you just ran from. All three merge together like one great floating head, culminating as the singular expression of your power. Your breath goes shallow. Like you are infused again with dolphin sense. Except with more edge and an appetite for revenge. You question your sudden lack of softness. The image fades, and you become fixated on a lawnmower – your head slowly follows it, and turns, but your body keeps going straight. Bam! You go down. Whimper. What was that? "Shit!" You are disoriented, scrambling with your hands and feet at the garbage you've spilled. Bottles scatter as you make your way back up. You jog-walk away from it, close to the edge of the road. The villas blush a full spectrum of pastel at you as you pass, and your temple pulses with a fresh outpouring of blood. You feel the turban get soaked. Bushes scratch your face and hands, the leaves prick you, they smell of fertilizer. The tang in your nostrils makes you gag.

Your feet burn, are hot, wet and stuck with stones and bits of glass. Blood and pus seem to squirt from multiple openings on the soles of your feet. You stumble, nearly fall, catch yourself on another useless wiry bush. Hold back tears. Hate this scene of black road and bubble-gum houses that never end. Your skin goes cold, then agonizingly hot. Then cold again. A trickle of sweat runs in a dead-straight line down your back. You have to get back there, to the ocean, to the drift-feel of darkness and swimming. Go straight there. To the cool easy pulse of your arms pushing through water. Gentle swift kicks. A straight path to water. Pull yourself together. You aren't sure you won't faint.

You close your eyes and wish hard for the serenity of the green snake's curling pathway. It was so graceful, looping its way into the kingdom of the jungle. For ten seconds, your head feels light and your heart free of any fear. But the drug pains crash in on you again, and sweat blasts through the pores of your body. Get it straight. You just got mixed up. You have to go straight to the bastard. To the source. Just get to the water and wash away all the cocaine. Get strong again. You pull at the gold dress, beg it to stop clinging to you that way. Finally you reach the bottom of the hill. A coconut-seller is hacking away on large green nut with his machete. A jovial group of work-ers are making their way up to Folly Road. Not down. Like you, but you are tripping on bloodied feet, drenched in sweat, itching like mad.

"The water, the water, it's okay, you're gonna be fine," scuffling along with your Hermès bag banging against your floppy ass, dropping it as you get near, your feet shushing through the sand, the sting of tiny grains in your wounds somehow exquisite. At the beach you throw yourself directly in. You close your eyes and let the cool saltiness take away all the hot salt from your skin. You lower yourself until your mouth goes underwater. The feel of getting clean of sand, of stones, of blood, of Folly fertilizers and flying bits of cut grass, of steely cars. Stop breathing. Go underwater now.

Bubbles erupt from your mouth. The turban unwinds and your hair inflates like a polyp of yellow cotton. A ribbon of pure red trails in a single, elegant strand alongside you. As you drift outwards, making soft dog paddles with your hands, the faces of the three men in your life loom up again behind your eyelids. The young man. The bastard. The man you nearly killed.

How strong you still are, you think. How capable. It's possible to be a free, glowing being buoyed by the sun and the immensity of the ocean. Look at you out here alone at dawn living off the sea in secret like a happy vagabond: eating food no one notices, wearing clothes nobody even remembers having, sleeping on luxurious boats, one after the next, without a soul finding a trace of you. Betrayal equals freedom, you think.

When something hard and waxen bumps you. You assume you've paddled your way into someone's surfboard, or boogey board. Or skiff with a silent motor attached. The last fits best with the tunnel of water you feel being tugged away from you. A small portion of the sea torn sideways. Right beside you. And then silently coming back into place. Rip then retreat. You blink calmly up at the sky as it comes into instant focus. Clouds split. And the words: do yourself a favour and run! Did you say that to yourself? Scanning fast, there is no boat anywhere near you. Your skin crawls, the faint hint of the sun's heat is gone and all you feel is an intense chill. You can't run on water, dummy Bunny. Calm down. But your heart has gone wild with some other memory, a physical one, rising up in you.

Then it bumps you again but this time harder. Stark awakening now, you see it. You bolt upright.

"Oh my god, no. No! It can't be that. Run Bunny, run Bunny, run!" you whisper. The ocean becomes like thunder roiling up, it seems to lick up around you in flames made of blood from your feet. Your feet. Your fucking feet. Run feet, run, you fucking bloody feet.

You try to run through the tumult of water but it's too deep. It's too hard. The heave of your thighs, you will them to plough through the heavy waves. Oh god, don't get me, don't.

And now on shore you see people coming to life. Tiny figures in the distance pointing at you, running towards you. They are too many impossible metres away from you. And in that flash of terror you recognize him: the young man is there sprinting across the sand.

"You bastard," you whisper as your face falls flat in three feet of water, and the shark – who is trying to figure out if you are edible, not what you taste like, but what species you are – bites off one of your feet.

And without any more interest, swims off in the other direction.

The splash of your body hitting shallow water. Then the thud of hitting the sand underneath. Then a cacophany of tiny splashes all around you and voices screaming and the slow single wave of blood, the last wave that washes all the way up over your body before the young man and a woman pick you up in their arms.

The ocean returns to a ripple of white caps. Then calmness as the car, with you in the backseat laid out as good as a corpse, tears off in the direction of the family lands.

///

"Which one is it?" Your voice is fragile, distant. Bright, hot daylight swirls around you through the car windows.

The upward view a relentless blue sky without clouds. "The right or the left?"

"Lady, you don't know?" says the woman. She's in the backseat with you, frantically tying knots with some kind of cloth. But her face keeps expanding and contracting and the sun is whiting out everything until it all turns black.

Then all around you, quiet blue: cerulean paint and warmish air flowing in different directions like long, soft hair.

"Up to both knees all I feel is fire." A large dry hand on your forehead.

"We picked you up lady, no one gonna take a person in your state to the hospital. You said it yourself, you got no insurance. No identity."

Warm hand heavy on your head. You are laid out on a bed in a house fortified by the background sounds of women. The walls are flimsy and the system of fans tremendous. You wonder if the house won't blow down.

"Here lady, here lady, we know what to do." She is touching the fire in your leg, doing and undoing things. You feel something rip, then seep, as if your leg is metal getting melted down. Your leg seems to run right out of you and onto the floor. When you close your eyes, you smell the sweat roll off the green arc of the snake as it releases itself from one position to the next.

"You had this bag with you, lady," she says. "You'll wear those pretty shoes again. Don't you worry about that." On the wall hangs an outfit you don't recognize, all frills and chiffon, bright red silk; not a dress, but a jump-suit for parties, with slits running all the way from the thighs down to the ankles, tied with ribbons. The ribbons have come undone on the left leg. A fan nearby makes the thin streamers of red silk flutter around the ankle's opening.

"It's my left foot, isn't it."

"That's right. Now you feel it, right? You lost your left foot to another world, lady. One foot here. One foot in the otherworld. In a way, you a very lucky, lady." You feel the woman's eyes looking at your closed lids and not ready yet to take in that strange thought, you fall asleep.

Day eight dead

(In which Miami is a mural.)

THE SCENE REPLAYS in your mind. How you told them you were once so protected. How, just a week ago, the sea glittered, reflecting a night field of stars that gathered into a singular beast that took you to shore instead of letting you be eaten alive. How instead of staying on land, you swam back to them, and hid. Swam and hid again. All of this comes out of your mouth like a slow string of bubbles as the two of them grunt and shuffle your deadened weight into their car. Beads of their perspiration spot onto your skin, and more from you pool on the plastic seating at your side. In the front seat they murmur politely, saying: "You're okay now." "Things will be well with you, lady." "I know her, she'll be fine." When the car slows to a halt, everything in view contradicts this: the unfamiliar shack that isn't a hospital, the two of them hobbling you towards its ramshackle veranda, your blood lighting up the whole side of the young man's pant leg, the look of terror in the woman who stands at the door, hands covering her mouth.

"But then, somehow, the bastard got me. He got me." The end of your story comes to you as a curiosity.

"Shhhh," repeats the woman, whose hands reach out to receive you, and you are lighter than air suddenly at her touch, and what you anticipate as hours of hysteria are instead hours of concentration, all around your lower half.

"No man can make a shark do that, lady."

You drift in and out of consciousness.

"Maybe you brought that shark to you."

Why would you do that? It's like some remarkable joke.

"And then he got me!" You yelp it out to the room.

///

Unknown bedroom, high in the jungle. The space expands endlessly in all directions, like the jungle has yawned in answer to you finally opening your eyes. They've forgotten my head, you think. Or my face. You feel the skin of your cheekbones edge its way back towards the openings in your ears. You are listening for the bones inside yourself. Wondering how the rest of you fared through the ordeal, because you ache everywhere, as though all your parts shifted around to the wrong locations. The solidity of your bones, and how they shiver, only reminds you of the stark absence of one of your limbs. You wonder about the body which you'd only really considered skin deep. So easily, gruesomely broken. By the shark.

What otherworld? Where are you, foot?

You open your eyes to the blue ceiling, wanting to speak to the shark, to ask, "Why doesn't it hurt? Why aren't I dead?"

The toes and the toenail polish, the tendons and bones and skin going into the mouth of another mammal. The notion almost makes you hysterical. You feel elevated. On some level you know you're drugged and thoughts spill out perilously. There is always one left if ever you want to measure how things are aging according to your feet, Bunny.

"I'll always have this other foot," you say, and laugh audibly. It draws a backdrop of women into the room.

You'd forgotten about them. They'd gone quiet for hours, for your sake, wanting to let you rest. They bustle into the small room, surrounding you from head to toe.

"Hi there, lady. You must be needing some water." A woman brushing your hair. Fans roaring up. Your eyes go to an opened window: bright swaths of palm leaves right there, practically entering the room. The oohing and ahing of a younger woman's voice,

"Gianni Versace. That's class." The girl in front of you holding up a single shoe.

"Where is the other?"

"Shhhh now, lady, never mind. We know you're a bit lost here. You told us all your story, all the trouble you been in. Where you were swimming and sleeping. You've been in a fever for days, but you're okay now, the drugs help it, and the new foot's being made right this second. You won't believe how beautiful it is. We're taking care of that foot. Or where it once was." She crosses herself. You feel the air whip around her fingers. "I said it already and I'll say it again: those shoes'll be on you in a week, no less! I'm Thule, by the way."

"Thank you, Thule," is all you can manage to say. Remembering the car and the young man tying your foot up in a sweatshirt.

You can't imagine what they're on about, the making of a new foot. You'll have to convince them to get you to a hospital is all. But then you remember: you have no identity cards to use in hospitals or for therapy or whatever else this kind of crisis involves.

Instead of worrying, you lap up the drugs and drink the small cups of water and soups that they bring you, and when you taste chicken in the broth it makes you happy in a very basic, futureless way. For now: just this blue house and its people, the jungle outside and the civet smell of the snake moving along the ground away from you, but then always back again to the window to watch you.

You close your eyes, comforted by the din of this extended family whose names you've all forgotten. Comforted by their fussing. It's always been you who's taken care, you who's fussed and served and made change and poured and undressed and sucked them off and wiped up afterwards and looked pretty again, no matter how tired.

///

Bunny, the cigarette girl. Cheap bunny ears on a hairband, bunny tail, cufflinks like a schoolboy's, and a bra stuffed three sizes too big. The raunch under your armpits and gathering in your underwear as you move through crowds of suits and their girlfriends. Girlfriends who sometimes befriend you but who mostly flash you looks as though to say, "I'd gladly tear your heart out."

Halfway though the shift you feel like a bad stain of electric blue moving across chintz carpets – electric blue being the colour of one of your costumes. Everything reeks of cigarettes even though you haven't smoked your whole life. Not yet.

"It's policy that you buy a Playboy lighter with every pack of cigarettes," you say with your young, tinsly voice. Your long blonde hair falls over their ringed fingers and gets caught in the spokes of the tray hinged at your neck.

Bunny, the card-dealer. You quickly advanced through the Playboy rungs, from cigarette girl to casino dealer. Here's where it got good. With the lacy white bib at your cleavage, standard issue for the girls who deal, you earned more respect from the clients. Plus you were a dash at counting cards: blackjack was easy, and throwing three decks at once didn't phase you. No sweat. Nothing bad happened. No victim stories. None from your girlfriends either, unless they never said. The men always treated you right. The men worshipped the hourglass frame that inspired them to win thousands.

You were good that way. You brought on the lucky streaks. Like the circle of dolphins protecting you. Wheeling around you. The spin of the wheel with chips thrown in by disembodied hands. Voices cheering. Bated breath. A gasp, and a hand to a chest. Then more whirls. Red. Black. White. More cheering.

Now green. The green spins so fast it obliterates the red, black and white. You frown. This isn't any game you know. Your heart tightens with fear, then the spinning slows, the green becoming familiar, and you wait in anticipation. And the snake swivels his head to look you in the eyes. "You left for awhile," you tell it. You follow the snake's movement to another table on the other side of the room. On its surface, shining instruments are laid out. Then held, one by one, by able hands. The long brown fingers of the doctor. Warm hands holding calipers, scissors, chisels, you don't know the terms. You smell bone and smoke. Skin flap over skin flap. Vessels and nerve endings being turned off like taps. It's a blurry view, but you see how they fold the end of your left leg into a shiny tapered baseball, but smaller, more like a very delicate horse's hoof.

The green snake looks you straight in the eye again. He doesn't want you to look anymore. He holds your eyes as if to say, "Stay here." So you can focus and not be too scared.

What is happening to your other foot, the right foot, the one that stayed in this world? It is massaged and measured, tipped to a certain toe-to-heel angle and held tight there. Your toes are spread open as wide as a little bird's wingspan. Then the foot is encased in something white and cold and puddingy.

Everything at the end of your body is electric and spinning outwards. Then all goes dull. The snake disappears out the window, blending in so well with the palm leaves you see it only by its movement. But you follow its winding motion, hypnotized by it, until you realize that at some point the right foot has dried in its case. It's become as cold and fixed as a crystal.

After you've slept for what feels like many days, the case gets cracked open. The foot of this land comes of its egg. "One egg for another," says the snake mysteriously, with its human-shaped mouth, its snake tongue pointing sheepishly out at you. It points to the left foot, the foot that is not of this land anymore, the foot that dissolved into the saliva of the shark's gullet and became part of the island landscape.

But the shark ate you by accident.

You felt it right there, tearing into the base of your calf. And into your heart. Into your chances.

What's left? Was it by accident?

"Right!" the snake corrects, giggling. "The stump looks like an egg!"

That night the shark swam as usual along the night tunnels of the sea. While you laid here, your foot disintegrated cell by cell inside some yellowish-red core, among some grey, gelatinous mess of inconsequential fishes and sea garbage. Poor foreign foot finding itself there. You pray it was consumed in one night, not more. Faster than battery acid, you pray. That it slipped from one state to another, from foot to sparkles, painlessly and without gore. As a ghost might pass through a wall. That it exited through the shark's skin and hung there above the beast, before kicking itself away. By way of more and more distant oceans. Escaping.

In your sleep you sense the snake enter the window, cross the floor and mount the bed. It slithers across your body, up your legs. Over your pelvis. There is something horrific and tantalizing about the snake's clean, dry movement over your hips. You groan at the thought of the young man and how you were once naked under his robe in that big glass villa. But this thought abandons you to the pain that takes over. Sudden. Excruciating. A crushing, burning, gnawing pain confused with a burning sensation around your hips, your pelvis, your vagina. You thrust yourself upwards, every lurking tingle from your foot passes up to your sex and culminates there. You don't even have to touch it – you are burned by the singular point of pleasure, the crepe-like hand that rubs you until you cum, a shudder so blunt and shattering it gives temporary form to your foot again, before releasing into a tiny wet stream.

And then it passes, the snake snaps like a flicked switch, and you understand that it was just a fantasy.

Sweaty, you turn your leg from side to side to be sure no phantom has stayed. "Nothing down there, nothing there at all," you say. The shark was a message to you, you tell yourself. That's all. The shark had its taste of you, but then let you go.

"Off you go now, back to the land," it seemed to say. Like it was bored by you. Like you had lingered too long in its territory, in ocean-time, when what you were supposed to be doing was making inroads back to where you once belonged.

"Sharks aren't that bright," tsk-tsks the snake, bringing you back into the focus of the room. "You think too highly of their motives. Most of their actions are blunders. There are others who will guide you now. Now you are a portrait of the intertwining of land and sea."

Your eyes wind around the double-helix made by the snake. He is seducing you now with this prospect.

Day nine dead

(The phantom's day.)

THE JUNGLE FALTERS in its peace, becomes a dank, crushing wilderness. Gruesome thoughts drip like pearls in your mind. They gather into hideous opaline shapes.

Whole. And now unwhole. Broken. Partial. Cut. You lift your head up from the sweat-ringed bed to look at the stump. You wag it up and down. Cringe. You think of a baseball bat gearing up for a game, but the bat is ragged and off-time. It lacks integrity. It is disgusting to you.

Mutilated. Unwholesome. Irreversible, a bloodied stump slopping all over the room.

Go back.

You can't get up on it, or walk on it. You gasp. Undo it. Go back.

I can't. A whistle scream inside each thought. The words fall like spittle, like coddled egg, then spin, then ram themselves up against your forehead. Breathe, breathe. Get out of here. Anywhere else. Be elsewhere. As you calm down, the burn becomes a presence; it moves steadily up your leg and grows into a singular flame ignited in your mind: you can go back. You can kill, set fire, slash. Kill off your whole self, not just the foot.

Then you imagine how that whole foot used to run under the table and up the leg of the bastard, or sometimes even up Coke-Bottle's leg. It depended on your mood. You feel the foot having a life of its own, a memory. The foot dares itself into the past, arches into a shoe, walks places, takes your weight. It's not yours anymore, but it is an entity circling the room, trying to find a place to land.

Foot, where are you?

How, in its last moments, it kicked so hard against the gaping mouth of the shark.

Let the absent foot go. Ignore it. Let it figure itself out.

You are alone. A breeze enters the room and flips a

doily halfway over a hairbrush sitting on the dresser. No sounds from the family anywhere in the house. Abandoned and silent, with the drugs draining out of your system, you fall into moments of pure void until the horrors rush in again. And the foot stands above the earth suffocating you, making you want to scream one last time. But after awhile you can only grunt. Whine. Moan. Then just stay still and feel nothing.

From a TV left on in the living room comes a deep, prophetic voice, surely an old movie:

. . . She was savage and superb, wild-eyed and magnificent; there was something ominous and stately in her deliberate progress. And in the hush that had fallen suddenly upon the whole sorrowful land, the immense wilderness, the colossal body of the fecund and mysterious life seems to look at her, pensive, as though it had been looking at the image of its own tenebrous and passionate soul.

She came abreast of the steamer, stood still, and faced us. Her long shadow fell to the water's edge. Her face has a tragic and fierce aspect of wild sorrow and of dumb pain mingled with fear of some struggling, half-shaped resolve. She stood looking at us without a stir, and like the wilder-

ness itself, with an air of brooding over inscrutable
purpose. A whole minute passed, and
then she made a step forward . . .

The flame of the phantom foot races up again from
the stump through your calf. It makes itself known. It is
stuck to you, you cannot kick it away. So you lie there
feeling its power set fire to the room, and you wait.

Day ten dead

(In which Bunny walks for the first
time without a foot.)

HAVING COME to count on being in this blue room indef-
initely, you hadn't foreseen what might come after: the
loss of euphoria and the petering out of the drug supply,
the image of the snake drying up within its own curled
form. But worse, your lost foot as the dark outcome of
some fitful and flawed plan carried out by the bastard.

Because the shark hadn't worked out, hadn't killed
you the first time. Not that the bastard could know that.

The paranoia of coming off drugs brings a cascade of questions. How can one man have power over creatures of the ocean? How did he know you'd tumble down into the sea that morning at dawn?

For what seems like days you've been resting, simply taken care of. No need to figure things out. Your foot wrapped up in impermanent injury, which you would sort out once you felt better. Once you were on your feet again.

You look up from an hour of staring at the palms, waiting for the snake to return with its message, and the young man appears. Your first impulse is to cry. He greets you like an old friend, not his lover.

"How you doin'?" You notice how his accent has shifted. How he carries his weight differently, his body more relaxed and in tune with the surroundings. You smell his skin as he leans over to adjust the sheet, a rich mix of clean sweat and soap. Everyone washes so often here, you've noticed.

"I feel like I'm nowhere. Or in somebody else's dream."

"Well that's good, I guess. No harm in floating for awhile. Lettin' it sink in, what happened to you. Do you understand it?"

"You mean, that I'm lucky I wasn't all eaten up?" You can't manage to smile so the young man is beaming on your behalf.

"Well everyone is considering you're special because of that, yeah. And that it was your foot that got taken. Here that means something."

From the abstraction of your talk with the young man, which is a comfort to you, to the material, grim reality: a foot, gone. It hits you again – it hits you because the phantom foot has reared up again, angled as it is in a furious clamp of pain.

"What could it possibly *mean*," you say, shaky and trembling, on the verge of tears. The young man puts a hand on your shoulder and you want more than anything to shrivel up so you're tiny enough to fit within that hand. "There is nothing *meaningful* about an accident that severs a body." Your words coming out tinged with venom even though you'd love to believe him. You'd love to return to the time when you thought the dolphins had chosen you, when you thought the sea was your ally and would never cause you harm.

"Well, they're sayin' it's a form of crossing over. But without having to go all the way. That you're supposed to stay in this world but now have access to some other place."

You have no idea what he could be talking about. "Hmmm," you mumble, noncommittal. If only you could get up and talk to him properly. His look is sympathetic, it pains you to not be able to get better from that look.

But you don't want his pity. And you can't help him to help you. So you prefer to be alone and, acknowledging your shooing hand, he nods on his way out, and you put your head in your palms and let yourself cry hard.

///

You are encouraged by the women, in particular Thule, to get up and move around with a crutch. So you take it from them, though wonder why they don't give you two. Why not a pair? They watch expectantly. As you become vertical, their hands dart out at you with each uncertain jerk of your body. For the first time in days you face the other side of the room. The back wall is covered in wallpaper of a Miami sunset. Two crooked palm trees in silhouette seem to be leaning out towards the pink ocean, as if their roots might give. Drips from the ceiling have stained the paper, and the corners pull away from the wall, showing gaps of blue paint behind it. You fix your eye on the ball of orange sun in the distant Miami scene – the place you were supposed to swim to, but didn't – as the white bulb, the egg of your bandage, swings violently, throwing you off balance. You slow down to reel it in, to make it lurch less.

"Fuck it," you whisper, grabbing at random the hands that flap and lunge at your sides, trying to catch you.

Their touch is light, their hold not altogether there, and they pull away, wanting to help you to find your own way. Verbal reassurances fly up around you and drift into the other rooms of the blue house. Through snatches of conversation you hear about "a foot that will come."

Whispered: "magic" and "lady." Then put together: "lady-magic."

"You just have to keep up your shape and your muscles," Thule is saying, as you hop a little, "so when the foot comes, you'll be ready to walk with the grace of a lady deserving like yourself. With your head high." Finally you lean on a young girl who, unlike the other women, is willing to take your weight.

Do they mean a prosthetic? Each time it's mentioned, they praise the maker so highly, show such reverence for him – her? – that you wonder if there isn't something more behind all this, perhaps a political motive? All you can do is nod and stare and agree. And wait. Several times a day you look at the bandaged hump but it is rare that you direct emotions of any kind, hope or anger – worst of all, humiliation – towards it. The doses of morphine help, but are infrequent, and you are weary of falling back into any drug-conditioned darkness.

Innocent white bulb, so quiet at the foot of the bed that you coo to it, tell it to shush, say it'll be fine. You feel the sparkling mass of stars taking the exact shape of the missing foot. Shut your eyes, let it tingle itself out, it will. It usually does. Then all, including the green snake who sits at your ear in these times, agree there is nothing there. That the foot has flown away. That it will lead the way.

The young man speaks little when he comes, but you hear him going over things with other family members in the kitchen, and then on the phone with his wife. He came here with his own concerns, private concerns, you remember.

To cheer you up he reminds you of the party on the island.

"You're still coming? Everything is on rush so that you can walk into that party on my arm." You hold his hand in yours and wonder why he cares so much.

Lastly, he hands you your NAUI card and walks back into the kitchen.

Day eleven dead

(In which Bunny dances.)

GREAT FANFARE IS PROMISED the day your new foot is to arrive – the same day the young man has invited his family over for a reunion.

The reunion is an extended family gathering, a celebration for the young man who has come home, finally, to choose his plot of land. You know of these lands: a span of beachfront, ancestral territory once owned by emancipated slaves, lands passed through generations until the entire area gained some quixotic, untouchable status. The law still can't intervene on family leases: they remain intricate, hidden, indecipherable. So the lands stay in family hands, even if, like the young man, the inheritor lived far from the island for decades. What matters is that you were born here. They say the island remembers all of its people, and that whenever a person once tied to the island returns, the island expands, makes more of itself. This time for the young man.

As things stir outside, you feel you begin to occupy a special place within the family.

You are helped into a bath. Thule props your leg onto a wooden chair and insists on washing your hair, at the same time soaping up your back with some scratchy mittens, then pouring hefty buckets of warm water over your head. You blink through the suds, refreshed.

"What about *your* friends, lady?" Thule says, scrubbing big circles up and down your arms now. "Or family?"

"My friends, well, wouldn't be able to come." That was clear. That line had been drawn. As for your sisters who live in the States, you don't know why you didn't try to contact them. It'd been so long. You thought you'd try to sort it out first your own way.

"No use calling them now, Thule. Try to get myself used to this new body first. To walking around and being on my own. It's not so bad, is it?"

"Nah, nah, you're gonna be just fine. But I'm not clear on where your home is, is all." She rinses your hair one last time. "Don't think about that today lady. We're thinking about it though, you should know that. You call me when you want out of this bath."

You nod to her. Your sisters wouldn't have a clue, is why. How to deal with the bastard or Coke-Bottle. The only solution would be to escape. But to escape at their hands, you couldn't take that: to be a dependent in some bourgeois house full of your nieces and nephews, where you'd have no purpose.

You draw the razor up over your good leg, fast, like you're used to doing it, but take it slowly around the left calf pushing the head of the razor in to get under the bandages. Wash your pits, then your privates.

You come out on the crutch to an army of beautifully adorned women. They seat you and comb the tangles out of your hair, put cream on you, cut and file your nails, get you into a new-looking bra and panties – someone must have bought them for you so you mouth a "thank you" to the group at large. The red silk jumpsuit hangs in the room like the poster of a once-loved celebrity. Obviously that's what you'll be wearing. They've decided. It's been pressed and the ribbons arranged along the leg to make neat thin bows – the last, you find as they pull it on over you, needs to be undone for your bandage hump to pass through. Lots of tsks, and "Never mind, we'll get it on." They want you to cooperate, to be a good sport. A young girl cuts through the primping hands with the blare of a hairdryer.

"Alright," you say, "go for it." She pushes your head forward, to position it upside down, and you feel the sting of metal heat at the base of your neck. Then hairspray and a stiff brush. The grandmother pours thick red Campari into glasses that the granddaughter passes around. You toss your head, your hair now a hot, blonde balloon. The taste of Campari puts you instantly in a good mood. A party mood.

"Ta-da! Now give us those toes!" The pretty young woman, who was so impressed by the shoes in the first place, leans over you, smelling of jasmine perfume. She paints your five toes in a red identical to the silk at your legs. Then your fingernails as well. You shake your head at her beautiful long fingers holding your worn, mottled hands.

"Oh." Wan smile. You'll be game, of course you will, but more and more you sense their togetherness, their belonging. That you are a temporary occasion, an accessory added to the excitement of having the extended family brought together into this jungle, their Elysium, a place of perpetual day. You hear chattering as a host of people surround the house, lighting paper lanterns and putting up string lights. The family resists how dark the jungle truly is, throwing light into every corner, each room radiating fluorescence and exposing the festive hues of the buffet: stewed meat, cabbage salads with vinegar dressing, deep-fried shrimp, tangy sauces, sweet alcohols, and Coke. Pursing your cherry-tinted lips you almost feel good. Really good.

When everyone has gathered inside the house, Thule, the young man and the doctor come to get you. You hear their happiness in the jaunt of their movements, how they bump about the tiny house. The jumpsuit flutters red around you as you enter with your crutch, the hands of your friends on your shoulders. The red distracts all eyes from the white bulb that hangs below you. Or they are polite enough not to look. A few people clap in anticipation directed at your other, whole foot, wearing the strappy silver Versace heel.

"We're thrilled to have you as our guest," the young man whispers. They seat you in a big La-Z-Boy against the wall. First there are drinks and a round of cheers. You feel the alcohol going quickly to your head. The room is full of enormous smiles, arms clasping other arms, laughing conversations and sudden whoops of glee. After awhile you find yourself alone with brightly clad buttocks as your global view. Then everyone drifts away from the area of the coffee table and is standing, conversing, feeling the music as it brings on a dance party. No one has talked to you beyond the initial flourish, to say hello or to ask how you've been feeling. What more could they say?

Food streams in from the hatchbacks parked out front and is served in gushes, on overflowing plates. The more they refill your plate, the deeper the La-Z-Boy draws you into its taut brown acrylic folds. The young man comes to you, saying, "You gotta try the ribs, the mashed potatoes, the jellied lobster." Licking his lips and looking skyward, far from you, he says, "It's been so long." Slapping his hand on his leg. "What do you say! Isn't this a party?"

You nod, mouth full of creamy potato. Before you can swallow, the young man is gone. He's left before you can ask him things you've been wondering about: how his wife is, how his land claim is coming along. Couldn't you both laugh now about the night you so recently spent together? You wanted to reassure him that you weren't attached and had no intentions of tying him to you now that you are . . . crippled. You shake your head and shiver, pushing the thought out.

You drift into a reverie that is as simple as staring at wallpaper. It has no content other than overlapping palm leaves blowing in a falling night, lanterns speckling the leaves with green, pink, red and blue.

Through a lacy yellow curtain that separates your room from the bright kitchen, you see Thule has gotten lost in the bliss of Campari. And you see a table full of rum, Jack Daniels and other bottles. Ordinarily you'd be right there with her, but you can't imagine hobbling past the curtain, or having a free hand to rest on the shoulders of people that block the way. Everyone is in motion. Couples are dancing. A woman is dipped Lindy-Hop style. Men and women are doubling over from jokes.

As the music gets louder you feel a twinge of desire mixed with panic. You too once loved to dance. You say thank you to the young girl who remembers you sitting there, who brings you drink after drink, who bends down to stroke your foot and admire your shoe. The absence causes a pang, and yet, the alcohol makes you think it isn't true. "It isn't true," you say out loud and the girl's eyes flash wide. When she runs off, inspired, returning an instant later with the young man, you see how the family and their guests share that look. How a light goes on inside of them, creating a brilliance that is collective, propelling them towards each other – to drink, to laugh, to encircle one another in their arms, to drift off contented and alone, casually stumbling down the steps to smoke in the cool of the twilit jungle.

Already, from afar, you've watched him talking intensely with other men, one pointing at an opened map. Your longing, in part, is to be him, to have a wide circle of family and community that believes you deserve a chunk of this island land. You are aware of so many of these plots just sitting here for decades with the wind blowing though them. The young man is smiling, his face animated with the prospects before him.

Then, mouth downturned when he gets close to you. "Oh my dear," he says, taking the drink from your hand and setting it down, lifting you forward so you feel his strength but also a slight unsteadiness in him. You want to trust him, to go fast into his arms and into the heat of the dancers. You forgive him for ignoring you for so long. As he lifts you off the La-Z-Boy, you feel a film of sweat that has made the jumpsuit stick to your back, and a gust of cool air sweeping against it. You put your entire weight onto the thin silver heel. Be a red flame cutting through the crowd, you think. At first you feel weightless and tingly. But your inner workings, your body's memory of itself, hasn't yet realized there is a major part missing. And the young man moves too fast, you have to remind him of your crutch, which makes him laugh so that he overcompensates. Finally he pushes you both through the throng, not as though floating like the others, but in some geriatric oscillation.

The young man enjoys the attention. The golden boy returned but now with the cumbersome flare of distress at his side. You feel him forgetting you as he plays hero, all teeth and glistening skin.

"Now we dance," he says, as neither question nor statement.

You nod, searching his eyes to see if he's truly still with you. But the crowd has conspired to approve of the young man's gesture to make the limbless woman dance. He takes you in his arms with careless ferocity and no one but the young girl notices the crutch drop to the floor. Cheers and more drinks poured. Your name, his name are chanted. He asks that you trust him completely: he will hold you tight and safe.

At times, you turn easily on the instep of the slim leather sole. Your right leg is still strong, a steadfast partner to the other leg which is loose and floaty, a trail of red ribbons leading down to nothing. He spins you gently, then more wildly as the crowd makes way. He acts sensitive, as if aware that you might get tired; he supports you, becoming the fallen crutch for the side of your body that's off-sync with itself and the room. From time to time he lifts you right off the floor, but the more he does this, the more he isn't looking into your eyes. His eyes glaze over, closing completely to feel the pulse of the music. Until someone changes the tune and the speakers blare out something he recognizes that sends a wave of thrill through him. A song from his childhood? His eyes are awake and seeing again, but in a way that makes him seem suddenly possessed by you – and you see how he looks right through you.

The crowd squeezes back in on your show. Their heat is electric. Each one of them is overtaken by the rhythm, and the voice of a woman that is languid, driving towards something guttural. From the corner of your eye you see the young girl standing guard, holding your crutch.

She is staring at you, brow furrowed, still as a pin, her supernatural eyes locked on yours, as if knowing that if she acts as a focal point you won't fall. Unable to hold her eyes any longer, you feel the swell of the family reunion lift you up, and the silver shoe lose the ground. He is gone. You have been passed to other hands, nudged along, so that you understand that each one wants a turn with you. Gentle, mostly smooth, first you are in the hands of those you recognize: Thule, then the doctor, who winks as he holds you, then the grandmother, who is surprisingly strong. Each time, your left arm is thrown around their arms, and your body hoisted in a small lift. But as you are relayed toward the kitchen, the crowd becomes younger, more raucous, less cautious. You feel the same mixture of trust and anxiety that you did with the dolphins, except this time in reverse order; the longer you float in this sea of bodies, the less nurtured and the more afraid you become.

A young woman misses her hold on you and you

stumble into the arms of a drunk man in a suit. He wants to make a show of it. Roughly grabbed, you feel your foot skid away, and you lurch forward, caught just in time by the young man who turns up and disappears just as quickly. Your balance leaves you for good as you heave to the side. Instincts tell you you will catch yourself, you always have before, but you fall onto nothing, no foot, empty space wafting around the hump and the flutter of red lines. You slip further into the slow-motion pulse of the room as you crash to the floor, the young girl's hand just missing yours – she's been running towards you – and the last thing you feel is her touch instead of pain.

"Oh, my dear!" The second time you hear this tonight. The young girl gone, the doctor now peering at you. His large warm hand is holding yours at the wrist, trying to read your heart. You notice the music has stopped. The light has gone sickly yellow. The room smells caged and sweetly sour. Foreheads are mopped with handkerchiefs amid the din of concern.

Invisible muscular arms raise you to standing. Half of your dress has turned a wet brown, it clings to your thigh. The young girl puts her thin arm around your waist and positions the crutch so you can finally lean on something that isn't someone, an object that will stand still under you. Your stump aches as you hobble your way back to the safety of the La-Z-Boy. There is talk of having "left it too late now." Some members of the reunion speak of going home. Thule's protesting voice: "But the other foot!" A squabbling as the young girl dabs at your thigh with a damp dishcloth, then takes the clean side and presses it against your temples. You feel a fever coming on. You drink water, hear apologies, promises about a foot on its way this very minute.

When the artisan finally shows, approaching you with solemn ceremony, carrying a shoebox in both hands, you hear a quiet respectful applause from the family now trying to sober up fast, an applause that drifts in and out of your consciousness so that you forget where you are. You imagine the claps to be the sound of waves slapping against the sea at night, and those waves sparkling with starlight and boat lights, and you see yourself swimming toward a tall white mast. On two able feet you step onto the ladder of the sailboat. The hoist of your voluptuous body out of the heavy waters, into the crisp night air, is really no more than the young girl having slipped the lever on the La-Z-Boy from upright to recline.

Day twelve dead

(The day a third foot is gifted.)

IN THE MORNING YOU WAKE to the sound of snoring, trumpet blares followed by soft retreats, like the flapping of elephant ears. You sense it coming from the row of rooms running one side of the house. For a moment you feel like something has shifted deep inside you. From the heat streaming in from outside you figure it must be deep into the morning. You feel unmoored from everything domestic, your body aches and feels sticky and you want nothing more than to douse yourself in the cool ocean water.

Off in the kitchen, the grandmother is silently moving bottles and glasses from one location to another. There is something eerie about her now, how her body hunches over. She is rocking from side to side but never getting very far.

Your eyes sweep over the dirtied hump. You won't look again. Not now. But the content of the glance, how it looked, stays with you: a rounded spectre, strung with dangling medical tape, streaked yellow and brown from drink stains. Like something someone from the Dark Ages would use to beat up someone else with.

When you try to focus instead on your other, pretty foot, also filthy, but well shaped, with bright red toenails flashing in the sunlight, a scream erupts from the absent foot. The feeling is so visceral all you can do is stare.

The grandmother comes into the room carrying a tray. As she hovers near, you smell the twang of coffee on her breath and pours some of the thick black liquid and passes you both cup and a shiny beige bun. She smiles a wide grin full of blackened teeth that look as if filed around the edges. You sip the sugary liquid and bite into the even sweeter bun. The sting makes your teeth whine. She lets you eat but is eager that you finish.

Her back is oddly very straight now, she primly sits

on the edge of a chair on the other side of the coffee table while her eyes flit continuously between you and the shoebox. The shoebox. You recall the face of the artisan: expectant, with lunatic eyes.

She wants you to open it. Without ceremony you pull off the cardboard top and plunge in, pulling out your gift: a stiff prosthetic other-foot.

It is grotesque and beautiful. Ancient and brand new at the same time.

The foot that puts you in the otherworld, the grandmother thinks with awe. You see it in her face. She gasps and claps her hands, golden light is sweeping across her wrinkled cheeks. But at the same time, something in her eye is contagious, and you are looking forward to the ceremony of this foot becoming part of you.

The grandmother swirls the air in front of her with both hands as if whipping something into being. She wants you to put it on.

How? She doesn't say, "Here, let me help you," but rushes toward you and the foot, undoing a system of leather buckles and brass clasps, a harness that reminds you of horse-riding gear. From it dangles an intricately carved wooden foot looking exactly like your own. The toenails are shaded with a hint of rouge. The foot is arched abnormally high, the grandmother already has the other silver Versace shoe on it.

It horrifies you, and also makes you want to laugh. Which you don't dare do, given the look of reverence on the grandmother's face. On some level you are grateful, but you have to pee and want to get up. Remaining silent, you let the grandmother start the process of unwinding your bandages. At that moment Thule stumbles out of a doorway. When she recognizes what's going on she calls out, "Wait, wait !" and runs the hallway, knocking on each door. Moment by moment, as the bandage comes undone, the family members awaken and sleepily encircle you.

Oohs and ahs over the other foot. Blearily staring at it, you think of the doctor saying you were lucky. Now you see that he meant lucky to have lost your original foot, the one that by now would be completely digested by the shark. The one that now needs to merge with this sculpted object, this thing in front of you that the family is presently stroking and poking at. You have to admit, when the family finally leaves it standing there freely on the coffee table, that the foot does have a magical, yet incomplete quality.

In order not to see the skin of your stump, which the grandmother bathes with water from a bowl, you study the otherworldly foot: its milk-stained finish made to match your skin colour, its familiar shape around the toes. A mimicry of your toes locked in static repose. A mirror-image replica of your right foot. Did the foot that got eaten alive actually look exactly the same as the right one? It doesn't matter. At a glance, and with the harness hidden under pants, the foot is deceptively real.

You heart leaps when you think: this foot will never age! And then crashes: how will I swim with this foot? A vast grin spreads across your face, imagining yourself kicking hard wearing the Versace heels. You get it now. No, no, the purpose of this wraithlike foot is to be worn to a party. Not the party of last night, but another party. The family has made you an otherworldly foot that will strut you into the bastard's annual bash. A foot to face the man at last. Just that.

Out of the bedroom steps the young man. Alone and blinking at you. You smile back, as the grandmother presses the wooden foot into place against your stump. It's a perfect fit.

Day thirteen dead

(In which Bunny blows up a superyacht.)

"Are you ready?"

"Ready."

The young man takes your arm and you make your first steps. It's four o'clock in the afternoon. Thule and the girls have spent the last hours doing your makeup, pressing your red silk jumpsuit, placing both your feet into the strappy silver sandals. But it is only with the young man at your side that you stand up and feel the full sensation of walking on your otherworldly foot.

Your hips wobble at first. You can't imagine letting your entire weight fall, even for an instant, onto the side where there is nothing but this garish, toy foot.

"Let it rest, let it rest there," encourages Thule. You cling to the right side of your body, the grounded part of you, feeling immoveable, stuck. "Go on," everyone seems to say at once, and as your weight comes forward onto the toe, you let your knee bend as it wants to do.

"Good, now kick it through," says Thule.

"Don't twist on the foot. Press your hips into it. That's the lady doin' it. Look at that."

And you feel no pain. Kicking it through becomes easy with each step, with each repeated motion you are reminded of your body as it once was, fluid and calm, pushing through water on the way to the next sailboat. So distracted by your immediate success and the thrill of being free again, you don't notice how your arm drifts out of the young man's grasp, or how your velocity picks up. Up and down the hallway you go, greeting the orange ball of the Miami sun as you pass it. In a swivel action that you marvel at, you meet the door at the far end of the kitchen, the door you first entered while bleeding like a stuck pig, and realize how much you want to exit it. You're rushing to get there.

"Whoa," says the young man, but you ignore him,

push his hands away. You feel yourself tipping forward too much, as if you might fall, but you are so hell bent on doing this you find a hold and catch your balance. The wood of the door is warm. You watch your silver-sandled alien foot lift itself as if disembodied from you. But still cooperating, it takes you over the threshold.

"Lady, nobody gets up on a wooden foot without days of practise. Look at you."

Look at me, you think. You walk feeling fierce and ready. Your agile card-dealer's fingers grip the ropes of the young man's muscly upper arms, but not for stability. You think of dancing with him that night. But more: you could go on your own now, if you wanted.

///

All that was known was that the bastard wanted to meet the young man, that he had a proposition for him regarding the young man's ties to the family lands. You were aware of the bastard's purpose, of the maps. What you might never know is why the bastard didn't include you, why he felt you had to be eliminated in his quest for more.

The boardwalk leading to the dock is strung with tiny, white lights. You grin at the fact that the party is being held on Jablonsky's superyacht, and that you are the mystery guest. As you jostle slightly down its three steps, you feel some doubt. Your foot has minimal bend at the ankle, and the young man adjusts, trying to make your gait more supple. You'd agreed the entrance would be seamless and ceremonial.

"You okay?"

"Okay," you say, but the anticipation of seeing the bastard eye to eye wells up in you like a storm.

You feel the young man's unwavering loyalty as he leads you through the crowd, which turns to look at you both as you pass. Beaded dresses parting as you approach, nighttime sunglasses tentatively lowered. In your periphery you see Coke-Bottle and Jablonsky turn, their shoulders joining in a twinned shudder. A glass of champagne hits the floor, its smash lost in the noise of the band. The ragged melody goes on and on. Like nothing is wrong, nothing has changed, drowning out the series of gasps as your identity comes into focus.

Then the tension behind all of the eyes not-seeing you, blocking your way should you want to jump overboard and out of this. But you don't really feel it anymore, the impulse is historic.

Now, like a sheet ripped open, the group parts and turns its back so that you walk alone with the young man along a strip of deck, toward the apex at which he, the bastard, stands, puffy-eyed and elegant in white.

His eyes flit for a half-second your way, the recognition

is there, you see it, the sort of recognition that will know you and deny you all at once. And then he carries on.

"Finally we meet."

"This is . . ." the young man begins to say, you've rehearsed it this way, that he would introduce you by your full name and watch the bastard cringe. But he stops, the three of you stay quiet.

The slow motion of taking in every inch of your husband. You are tall in Versace. You look at him eye to eye. He has aged. The breeze has undone his careful combing, his hair sits up like a flimsy box on top of his head. A hint of a smile crosses your lips. He sees it and coughs.

You catch a movement across the deck, the split-second flash of a woman at the rails, tossing her hair, and you know: it's Her. The bastard's new girl. A version of you. But younger.

And suddenly you feel the great weight of yourself and the familiarity of your man right there in front of you and you want to reach out to him. To take his hands and pull him into you.

And you read in his eyes a blank ferocity, and the sting you feel deepens as his hair falls into a position you know and love, and his face shifts, taking on a quizzical look of pride – for the woman he once adored, then killed off. Tried to kill off for reasons only the two of you alone will ever know, but you managed to survive against all odds.

The respect is palpable. He almost sees it as a testament to his own ruthlessness. He dares you to challenge the bulletproof script in his head, the one he switched around on you, the new one which he has repeated to himself over and over, as to why you were erasable, why this situation was exceptional, how he is exceptional, even rare. "No, no, Bunny, you have not been replaced, my darling."

Toss of lush blonde hair in your periphery. It might as well be a photograph of you two decades ago, pushing your butt out to the crowd, having a cigarette break between deals. The smoke spins outwards, away from her beauty, and you feel her youthful confidence, a confidence that sears. "It's all our lot, lady, get over yourself." The plotlessness of competing with this unknown woman. You shift your weight to the new left foot. A pain erupts there: an ecstatic tide soaring up through your leg. Your eyes turn to slits that hold the bastard's gaze, but then soften, and you look at him as you always would have. A plain and simple look between two people who have known each other a long time. His eyes drop and he sees your beige foot. His lip curls at the sight of it. He turns away to the rails. The blonde is fiddling with her purse.

It's okay, I get it, you don't see me. You're disgusted.

You laugh a little, though not at him.

A squeeze from the young man.

One last meaningful look at the bastard and you follow your impulse: to lean in to kiss him goodbye.

The moment is suspended, to be recorded by everyone who watched: how you fell a little too deeply into each others' embrace, to the point of forgetting all falseness. Fell so that your vision of a wall of flames transporting the superyacht into the island's history books of Epic Accidents prophetically encircled you and him first, concealing a kiss like a fugue, like a tsunami which couldn't even touch the firewall containing and exposing the love within your hate, and how in that transcendent state the stiletto of your Versace accidentally stepped on the bastard's slipper and pierced both shoe and foot all the way through. You didn't feel a thing because, naturally, it was the otherworldly foot's doing.

You see tears shroud his eyes. He leaves you and walks to Her. As he reaches her side, half-stumbling into her arms, you watch it take shape: a cartoon-sized teardrop painted blood red by the coloured bulbs of the band's lighting system.

Your heart hardens and then, strangely, opens itself to the night air and the clear view of the prow skimming over the black waters towards an even blacker horizon. The yacht has already long pulled away. The crowd of friends and acquaintances are following the bastard's lead. You are there, but to be ignored. The tension is thick and emboldening in the way that exile is beyond solitariness. It makes you fearless. Only the neutral figures, the waiters, don't know to ignore you, and they bring you glass after glass of champagne, which you sip but mostly throw out to the oncoming waves. The young man left your side long ago, though you do see him looking down at you from the upper deck and you share a look of complicity. His eyes flash in recognition: of the euphoria, at some freedom you share. At the wildness that has overtaken you. And somehow his is a more ancient understanding of what it means for you to wear the otherworldly foot. Even though, you think, he is still too young to know.

As you turn to the prow, where the mist is rising, a vision intervenes: a wall of fire lighting up the ocean. Behind that wall, a thrash of swimmers moving in every direction into the invisibility of the night.

You nod into the mist long enough for it to make a film of saltwater on your face. You'll make sure the young man gets away on the dinghy, you know it's there.

Your shoe sparkles in the moonlight. A dagger. Holding the rail, you sway it this way and that, gyrating your hips to the music, digging your heel into the deck to feel out your weight. Majestic and robust. The foot radiates melodic power. It knows the music better than you and now you are its vehicle.

Confusion, then horror from the sidelines as you let go of the rail and dance openly, wildly, and deeper into the space of the decks. The percussionist spurs you on with her beat, she plays into your awkward movements, matching your strides as they clip, then fall, then catch. Gasps break out and someone reaches out to stabilize you. You feel arms grabbing at you, which you bat away but also fall into, you are tossed from old friend to old friend. You see their eyes, concerned or terrified, and their jeweled hands fumbling for you or pushing you away, not wanting to touch you. You are aware of a contrast in your skins. Theirs, silky and maudlin, encumbered by links of gold chain, while yours is strident, burred, as if you'd grown a layer of rough hair. In your mind, you lick their arms. Kick them with your lurid prosthetic. Their drinks crash to the floor as you bump and falter and flail, you are dizzying them within your extended power of the music gone wild. You feel the young man, distant but there, smiling, as the drummer's grin grows from wide to enormous. Some of your old friends are getting into it, they like it even, and approach you again and again until you find them in the mass of bodies.

It is then that you pitch yourself against the bastard's girl, who screams when you touch her. In that second of contact, you smell your scent roll away from you onto Her. Pagan sweat washing over Dior Poison perfume. You want to drown Her with the reek of you, the horror of you, to rub your own nose into the young bulbs of her tits that bust out of her dress. In a way, you kind of love Her. Want to warn Her.

"Only one woman on the raft," you say to Her as she weakly brushes you off.

It will be a night fire. The ropes cut free.

A sunrise rescue.

Jablonksy is there, smiling at you. And she nods. You nod back at her. The young man is there. He takes your hand and pulls you away from the dancers who have forgotten you. Now it's the drummer girl who hammers their bodies into a Dionysian state, you laugh and mock high-five her, as your old friends throw off their jackets and stamp on the broken glass. Even Coke-Bottle. Even the bastard's girl. Only the bastard watches you with dead eyes as you lean into the young man's arm to go down the narrow stairs into the galley. On your last step you turn and see the bastard limp off, a spittle of dried blood marking his slipper.

"Here, eat this." The young man feeds you their lobster and their caviar, butter and blackness dripping from his fingers into your mouth. You gorge on their hors d'oeuvres, ripping cellophane off the platters, letting blots of mushroom sauce and sizzled potato fall all over the galley floor. You gulp down their bubbly. All of it drips from both your mouths as you laugh and kiss and then laugh so loudly the staff runs in the other direction.

But reporting you is pointless. You are a ghost of flesh now and into forever. You cannot catch me, you think.

acknowledgments

For informing my research, I wish to thank Amy E. Potter for her graduate dissertation entitled *Transnational Spaces and Communal Land Tenure in a Caribbean Place: "Barbuda Is for Barbudans"* (Graduate Faculty of the Louisiana State University, Doctor of Philosophy, 2011).

The excerpt on p. 121 is from Joseph Conrad's *Heart of Darkness*.

Thank you to the Canada Council for the Arts, le conseil des arts et des lettres du Quebec, and to Passa Porta: la maison internationale de littérature a Bruxelles for the support and production of this book.

Thank you to my publishers Jay and Hazel Millar for their respect and enthusiasm, and to my editor Malcolm Sutton for his great investment in me as a writer.

For other close-reading, editorial and other killer advice, I am grateful to Kathleen Piercy, Kyla Brueciani, Devlin Kuyek, Benny Nemerofsky Ramsay, Kristian Bakkegaard Andersen, Carmen Joy King, and most of all, to Caia Hagel.

Sending adoration from afar to my aunt Darlene who hosted me through the years in her home in the Caribbean, and who, two years ago, reminded me that if you are open to it, the place you travel to has a story of its own to tell.

I wish to thank the darkness of time when I wrote this book to "Thirteen Angels Standing Guard 'Round the Side of Your Bed" blaring late into the night in my kitchen in Brussels. And to Manuel, for holding my hand many months later, through a lighter time, in order to finalize the chapters.

And to my family: Kathleen, Jay and Liz (and their boys), Una and Fanon, my angels, I thank you for your help to me in the final stages of writing this, and I dedicate this book to you.

colophon

Distributed in Canada by the Literary Press Group www.lpg.ca.
Distributed in the United States by Small Press Distribution
  www.spdbooks.org.
Shop online at www.bookthug.ca.

Set in Portrait • Type and design by Malcolm Sutton • Edited for
the press by Malcolm Sutton • Cover by two thugs.